Rusty

Mr. Crow

Tom

Dominic

Quinn

Meeka

me!

Stacy

My
Best
Frenemy

Friends for Keeps

My Best Frenemy

Julie Bowe

Dial Books for Young Readers

an imprint of Penguin Group (USA) Inc.

My thanks again and again (and again!)
to illustrator Jana Christy;
my agent, Steven Chudney;
and my editor, Kathy Dawson

DIAL BOOKS FOR YOUNG READERS
A division of Penguin Young Readers Group
Published by The Penguin Group
Penguin Group (USA) Inc., 375 Hudson Street, New York, NY 10014, U.S.A.

Penguin Group (Canada), 90 Eglinton Avenue East, Suite 700, Toronto, Ontario, Canada M4P 2Y3 (a division of Pearson Penguin Canada Inc.) • Penguin Books Ltd, 80 Strand, London WC2R 0RL, England • Penguin Ireland, 25 St. Stephen's Green, Dublin 2, Ireland (a division of Penguin Books Ltd) • Penguin Group (Australia), 250 Camberwell Road, Camberwell, Victoria 3124, Australia (a division of Pearson Australia Group Pty Ltd) • Penguin Books India Pvt Ltd, 11 Community Centre, Panchsheel Park, New Delhi - 110 017, India • Penguin Group (NZ), 67 Apollo Drive, Rosedale, North Shore 0632, New Zealand (a division of Pearson New Zealand Ltd) • Penguin Books (South Africa) (Pty) Ltd, 24 Sturdee Avenue, Rosebank, Johannesburg 2196, South Africa • Penguin Books Ltd, Registered Offices: 80 Strand, London WC2R 0RL, England

Text set in ITC Esprit
Printed in the U.S.A.
1 3 5 7 9 10 8 6 4 2

Library of Congress Cataloging-in-Publication Data
Bowe, Julie, date.
My best frenemy / by Julie Bowe.
p. cm.   (Friends for keeps)
Summary: Almost-ten-year-old Ida May finally has a new best friend at school, but after bossy Jenna Drews starts an increasingly dangerous game of Truth or Dare, Ida is not quite sure who her friends really are.
ISBN 978-0-8037-3501-9 (hardcover)
[1. Best friends—Fiction. 2. Friendship—Fiction. 3. Truth or dare (Game)—Fiction. 4. Behavior—Fiction. 5. Schools—Fiction.] I. Title.
PZ7.B671943Mw 2010 [Fic]—dc22   2009025099

For Micah, my daughter and friend for keeps!

My
Best
Frenemy

Chapter
1

I'm Ida May and you probably think that I'm skipping school, because it's 9:00 on Wednesday morning and I'm not there.

Skipping school is something I hardly ever think about doing. Not unless my best friend, Stacey Merriweather, passes me a note during silent reading that says she is desperately craving fresh pineapple and maybe we should fly to Hawaii right away to get some.

I'm not crazy about fresh pineapple, like Stacey is. Not like Jenna Drews is, either. Jenna is crazy about anything that grows inside a prickly skin. But she would never skip school to get it because she is even more crazy about following the rules.

Still, me and Stacey might ask our teacher, Mr.

Crow, if we could use the classroom computer to silently read about Hawaii. And while we were reading about volcanoes and tidal waves and hula dancers, we might secretly click over to the airplane ticket page and see how soon we could fly there. And how much it would cost to buy two tickets. Plus a pineapple.

But I'm not skipping school today, or even pretending to. I'm still in bed because it snowed a bunch last night and so my whole town, Purdee, Wisconsin, is under a puffy blanket, just like me. Today was supposed to be our first day back after the holiday break, but because of all the snow we get a bonus day off.

My mom brought me breakfast in bed to celebrate. Hot chocolate and gingerbread people. Me and George are sharing the cookies, but I get most of them since sock monkeys don't eat much.

"How about an arm, George?" I ask, dunking a one-armed cookie into my hot chocolate until it's soaked up to the neck.

George does not reply.

"A head then?" I ask, biting off the soggy arm.

Still no answer.

4

"One stomach for sale," I sing, making the headless, armless gingerbread person dance in front of George's black button eyes. "Going once . . . Going twice . . ."

George glances away.

I shrug and bite the cookie down the middle.

George isn't as interested in cookies as he used to be, back when I was little.

I push off my blanket and pop two legs into my mouth. Then I set my mug on my nightstand, right next to a picture of me and Stacey Merriweather. We're making goofy grins in the picture because that's what best friends do when someone says, "Smile for the camera, girls!"

Stacey is my one and only best friend. Maybe if I was taller or wider or louder or prettier I would need more than one so I could spread myself around more. Like Brooke Morgan. She's the prettiest girl in my fourth-grade class at Purdee Elementary. She's also tall. And kind of loud. It takes a lot of friends to soak her up.

But not me.

And not Stacey.

We're happy with one best friend each.

A gurgling sound comes from my dresser. That's because a fish tank is sitting on top of it. It was a Christmas present from my grandma May. She lives in Tacoma, Washington, which is a long way from Purdee, Wisconsin, so she only gets to visit me once a year. That means I usually get good presents from her.

A little motor hanging over the side of the tank pumps bubbles into the water and a filter inside it sucks the fish poop out. I like the gurgling sound even though it took me a few days to remember it's coming from my new fish tank and not from some creature living in my closet.

I got a goldfish too. It's swimming around a pirate skeleton that's leaning against a fake treasure chest on the bottom of the tank. The pirate skeleton has a hidden tube that pumps air through its bony arms, which lifts a jug to its mouth. The jug says RUM on it. Personally, I'd rather lift Choco Chunks to *my* mouth, but I don't think pirate skeletons are much into chocolate.

There's also a pair of old dentures on the bottom of the tank. They came from my dad's orthodontist office, not my grandma. They're kind of creepy, but sometimes I like creepy things. Like when me and Stacey go to the *National Geographic* website and dare each other to stare at the close-up photos of sand tiger sharks and anacondas and jumping spiders and cane toads. Stacey actually thinks the cane toads are *cute*. But not me. Sometimes their buggy eyes and shiny skin fill me up with so much creepiness, I'm in danger of peeing my pants.

"Come and get it . . . um . . . fish," I say, sprinkling food into the tank. I haven't thought of a good name for my goldfish yet.

Actually, he's more of a *splotch*fish than a *gold*fish. That's because he's covered with white, black, and orange splotches. Like maybe the pirate skeleton got a little carried away with finger paints.

I tap on the tank and practice a few names on him. "Here, Frank," I call.

My fish swims behind the dentures.

"Charlie?" I try next. "Is that your name?"

He swims to the far corner of the tank and nips at floating flakes.

"How about Halibut?" I ask.

No reply.

"Lazibut?"

Still no answer.

I sigh. Fish are about as talkative as sock monkeys.

I walk over to my nightstand and pick up a narrow box of oil pastels that's sitting next to the picture of me and Stacey. Oil pastels are like crayons, only better. I got them from Santa, along with a pair of paintbrush barrettes.

There's a picture of a real artist on the back of the box. You know she's a real artist because she's holding an oil pastel stick up to a big easel like she's getting ready to draw a really great picture. Like me and Stacey do sometimes. Under her photo it says: *Arielle Lafayette, Award-Winning Artist,* which is another clue.

Extra-Fine Quality Oil Pastels: 16 Colours is printed on the front of the box. *Colours* is not spelled wrong. It's spelled artistic.

The box makes a nice sound when I slide it open. Like when you slide your arm into a new smooth shirt. There are sixteen sticks inside it. They make a very organized rainbow. *Rouge* for red. *Jaune* for yellow. All the sticks have artistic names.

I take out *bleu clair,* which is really just light blue. Then I pick up my sketchbook, find a clean page, and draw hills covered in light blue snow. You might think they should be white, but snow can be lots of different colors, depending on how you look at it. Once, when me and Stacey went sledding, it even looked like it was covered with silver sprinkles.

I'm hunting around for a pencil so I can draw me and Stacey sledding on the blue hills, when I find something else instead. A little book that has been sitting on my nightstand since the start of our holiday break. It has a purple cover with the word *Journal* printed on it in curly cursive letters. There's a pen clipped to the cover. It's also purple and when you press down on the tip, the whole thing lights up. I think they do that to make you want to write more.

I would rather draw than write, but I guess Jenna Drews isn't aware of that fact or she wouldn't have given me the journal and the pen. She was my Secret Santa at school. When I opened my gift from her at our holiday party I thought, *Thanks a lot . . . ho, ho, ho,* but then Jenna showed me how to make the pen light up, so I felt a little bad about not liking it at first. I said thank you to her and I mostly meant it.

Quinn, on the other hand, did not say thank you for the Secret Santa gift I gave to him. Even though Mr. Crow kept reminding us to say it. And even though I gave Quinn a mini basketball (which did not light up, but it did make burping sounds when you bounced it). Quinn bounced the ball like it was the best gift in the world, but when Mr. Crow gave him the reminder, all he did was glance at me and grunt.

Boys.

On the first page of the journal is a note from Jenna.

Ida,
    I hope you like this journal which I gave to you at our fourth grade holiday party.
    I also gave you a pen.
                    Jenna Drews

Maybe I should tear out the first page, because who wants a used journal? But then I get another

10

idea. I pick up an oil pastel stick and draw a picture of Jenna instead. It's not a mean picture exactly, but I do give her a very *rouge* mouth. And I make her *jaune* braids curl up like Pippi Longstocking's. Then I write: *Jenna Drews, Boss of Fourth Grade* under the picture, which is not being mean. It's just being true.

Brooke should be next to Jenna because they have been best friends since kindergarten, but this is my journal, so I draw a picture of *my* best friend instead. Dark curly hair. Half-moon eyes. Big sparkly smile. I write: *Stacey Merriweather, BFF* under it.

You're supposed to start with "Dear Diary" when you write in a journal, but sometimes I don't like to do what I'm supposed to. Besides, no one in the world is named "Diary," so what's the point of writing to them?

Maybe I could write to a pretend person, like in a book. I glance at my bookshelf and see the new books my aunt Margo gave me for Christmas. Mostly chapter books, but a couple of little-kid books too. She gives them to me because of the good pictures.

One of the books is called *Stellaluna,* which is about a bat, not a person. Normally, I'm not a big fan of bats even though they *are* a tiny bit cuter than cane toads. But the pictures are good. The story is pretty good too, because even though Stellaluna *is* a bat, you can learn to like her.

Turning to a blank page, I make the purple pen blink against my chin.

I'll write to Stellaluna.

Stella for short.

Dear Stella,

How are you? I am fine. This is the first time I have written to you so here is a little background information.

1. I am a girl.
2. I am 12 minus 3. (Get it?)
3. I have bleu clair eyes.
4. I do not have freckles.
5. Or pierced ears.
6. I really want to get pierced ears, but my parents say I have to wait until I'm old enough to take care of them. I'm not sure how old that will be, but I know it will have double digits.

7. My best friend is Stacey Merriweather.

8. My second best friend is my sock monkey, George. Please don't tell George he came in second.

9. My regular friends are Randi, Brooke, Meeka, and Jolene.

10. Jenna Drews (see page 1) is not exactly my regular friend. She used to be my enemy, but now she's not exactly that either. I guess you could call her my frenemy.

11. I don't like writing much.

12. I don't like boys much either. Except for my dad. And Mr. Crow. Tom Sanders is okay too. He's the only boy in my class who doesn't burp on a regular basis.

13. And maybe I like Quinn.

14. A little.

I put that last part in because you are supposed to tell secrets in a journal. Sometimes I do what I'm supposed to.

Chapter

2

Here's the thing about snow days. They're fresh and fun in the morning, but they start to go bad and boring in the afternoon. So, after lunch, I call Stacey to see if she wants to go sledding. Sledding is the only sport I'm good at. Everyone calls the sledding hill in town *Ricochet Ridge* because it has lots of bumps to keep you on your toes.

Kelli answers the phone. Kelli is Stacey's mom, but you don't have to call her Ms. Merriweather or anything.

"Stacey isn't here, Ida," Kelli tells me. "She got snowed in at her dad's and won't get back until tonight."

"Darn," I say. "Will you tell her I called? And that I can't wait to see her?"

"Will do," Kelli says. "Have a fun snow day!"

"I'm trying," I reply.

I start reading one of my new books, but I am so much wanting to talk to Stacey that I ask my mom if I can call her at her dad's house, even though that feels a little scary. Her dad or her brother might answer the phone and I don't know them at all because they live in another town and Stacey lives here with her mom and grandma.

"Okay," Mom says, handing her cell phone to me. "But keep it short. I'm low on minutes."

I call Kelli back to get the number. Then I drink a glass of water because my mouth gets dry when I have to do scary things and right now it feels like sidewalk chalk.

I press the numbers on the phone.

"Hello?"

It's Stacey. I do a big breath of relief.

"Hi," I say. "It's me. Ida."

"Ohmygosh!" Stacey says. "Ida! I'm so glad you called! I'm sooooo bored!"

"Meeeee too," I say back. "Now we can be bored together. But only for a little while because my mom set the timer."

"Have you seen any of the others?" Stacey asks. "Brooke? Meeka? Jolene?"

"Nope, nope, and nope," I say. "I saw Randi one day at the Purdee Good Café, but she was hanging around Rusty and some of the other boys, so I mostly pretended I didn't see her."

"It's so not fair that I'm stuck a million miles away from everyone," Stacey says.

Stacey isn't really a million miles away. Sometimes she likes to make her stories sound bigger than they are.

"If you were here, we could go to Ricochet Ridge," I say. "Or build a snow fort. Or make maple syrup snow cones like Laura and Mary Ingalls did when they were pioneers on the prairie. They sound yucky, but still."

Stacey giggles. "Maple syrup snow cones. That sounds like something Jenna Drews would like."

Jenna and her family like to eat lots of naturally yucky things. Like tofu and spinach and wheat germ. I don't understand how something with a last name like *Germ* can be good for you.

I giggle too. "She's probably setting up a snow cone stand in her yard right now."

"And *making* people pay fifty cents to eat them!"

We both giggle until we snort.

"I can't wait to show you what I got for Christmas," I say, thinking about my box of oil pastels. Stacey knows how much I like to draw, so she will for sure be excited for me.

"Me too!" Stacey says. "I got tons of clothes and stuff." Stacey runs down her whole list. "What did you get?"

"I'm keeping it a secret until tomorrow," I say.

"But I'm your best friend," Stacey says in her frowny voice. "You're supposed to tell me your secrets."

I think about my secrets. Only one, really. The one I wrote in my journal about liking Quinn.

"Okay," I say. "Here's one. I got a pet fish."

"Cool!" Stacey says back. "What else?"

"Let's see . . . I got a journal from Jenna."

"That's no secret," Stacey says. "I was there when she gave it to you."

"Yeah, but you didn't know I started writing in it."

"You did? What did you write?"

Part of me wants to tell Stacey what I wrote,

17

but another part of me likes the squirmy way it feels to keep my secrets to myself. "Sorry," I say. "That information is classified."

"I bet you wrote about your *crush,* didn't you?" Stacey says. "Who is it? Joey? Rusty? Quinn?"

"Nope, nope, and—"

The kitchen timer starts beeping. "Oops," I say. "That's all we have time for today."

"No fair!" Stacey says.

"Sorry," I say. "The timer has spoken. Find me as soon as you get to school tomorrow, okay?"

"Okay," Stacey says. "Be prepared to tell me *everything.*"

I giggle. "You too."

I turn off the timer and think about calling someone else to go sledding with, but the only other phone number I have belongs to Jenna Drews. My mom has to call her mom sometimes because they're both on the PTA. Plus, after Jenna's dad lost his job, my mom and Mrs. Drews talked a lot because things weren't the greatest over there. But now Jenna's dad has a job again, and even though Mrs. Drews had to get a job too, things seem better.

I decide to go to the sledding hill alone, hoping there will be at least one other girl there.

There's a bin of warm winter clothes by our front door. I start putting stuff on. Wool socks. Purple snow pants. Striped scarf. Pink hat with a fuzzy yellow tassel. I zip up my snowflake jacket and pull on my clunky boots, which make my feet look like capital L's. I tug on a pair of black gloves. A minute later, I tug them off again because it's hard to turn a doorknob with gorilla fingers.

My orange plastic sled is on the porch. I grab it and clunk down the steps before I sweat to death.

My dad is shoveling the sidewalk in front of our house. He came home from his job early because the snowstorm made his patients cancel their appointments. Dad may be an orthodontist, but he still hasn't fixed my crooked teeth.

"Hi, Ida," Dad says. He leans against the handle of his snow shovel. "Coming to help?"

"Sorry," I say. "Just passing through." I leave deep footprints in the unshoveled snow as I scoot around him.

"Ah, c'mon," he says. "I'll make it worth your while."

I stop and turn around. "How worth it?"

My dad studies the snow that's still drifted across the sidewalk. He rubs his whiskery chin. Every winter my dad grows a beard and every spring my mom makes him shave it off. "How about a dollar's worth?" he asks.

"Dad, that's worse than the Tooth Fairy."

"Okay then," he says, "how about five dollars?"

I study the sidewalk and rub my chin too. "How about . . . fifteen?"

My dad grins behind his mustache. "How about ten?"

I study the sidewalk again. "Will I get in trouble if I say no?"

"No," Dad says. "But you'll get *ten dollars* if you say yes."

"What will I get if I go sledding now and build you a *snowman* later? A big one, with aluminum foil braces in its mouth. And a sign in its stick hands that says, *For a warm smile, call May Orthodontics.*"

Dad laughs. "That will get you my sincere thanks. And a cup of hot chocolate."

"Deal," I say, and head down the partly shoveled sidewalk.

As soon as I get to Ricochet Ridge I see lots of kids, but it's hard to tell which are girls and which are boys because everyone looks pretty much the same covered in snow. Then I see one girl for sure.

Two, actually.

Jenna Drews and her little sister, Rachel.

As soon as Rachel sees me she smiles and waves. I smile and wave back. Rachel is a lot friendlier than her sister.

"Hi, Ida!" Rachel calls. She waddles up to me. Kindergarteners always waddle when they wear snow boots.

"Hi, Rachel," I reply. "How's the sledding?" I look up at Ricochet Ridge and see three kids wipe out on saucers. Another kid comes down the hill on a sheet of cardboard and runs right into them. A monkey pile on an inner tube tumbles into them next. They all come up spitting snow and laughing.

"Fast," Rachel says.

"Like always," I say back.

"Is that your *sled*?" I hear someone say. I look up and see Jenna walking toward us. Her cheeks are the same color as her bright red hat. Her blond braids stick out under it, stiff with snow. She's pulling a toboggan. It's made of shiny wood and braided rope and probably a lot of other natural things.

I look behind me at my orange plastic sled. Then I look at Jenna. "Yep," I reply.

Jenna gives my sled another glance. Then she pulls her toboggan between us and stands it up on end. "This is *my* new sled," she says.

"It's mine too," Rachel adds.

"Whatever, Rachel," Jenna says. "You can take turns with Ida."

"Um . . . thanks," I reply.

It's a long walk up Ricochet Ridge, especially when you are dragging a sled and wearing capital L boots. When we finally get to the top, I turn and look down. I gulp a little because I always feel braver when I'm standing at the bottom of the hill looking up than I do when I'm standing at the top of the hill looking down.

"I'll steer," Jenna says, taking the front seat on the toboggan. She picks up the loop of rope that's attached to the curved wooden front and holds it with both of her mittened hands. "Get on, Ida," Jenna says. "Rachel can use your sled."

"You can go with Jenna first," I say to Rachel. "I don't mind. Really."

"That's okay," Rachel says. She plops down on my sled, belly up. She looks like a pink turtle with an orange shell. "Push, please!" she says.

I nudge the sled and Rachel squeaks over the edge of the hill. Her boots cut grooves in the packed snow as she slips away.

Jenna shakes her head. "She *always* drags her feet." Then she pumps the toboggan rope like horse reins. "Come on!"

I climb on behind her.

"Tuck your feet under my legs so you don't slow us down."

I don't like the way Jenna bosses me around, but I do like sledding, so I tuck my feet.

"Push off!" she shouts.

I dig my knuckles into the edge of Ricochet Ridge and push as hard as I can.

"Harder!" Jenna shouts, rocking forward to work up some speed.

"Need a hand?" I hear someone say. I turn and see Tom Sanders standing behind us.

"Yes," Jenna says to Tom. "Ida's not strong enough. Go get one of the big boys to give us a push."

I roll my eyes.

Tom gives me a grin. "Hang on," he says.

I grab Jenna around the waist.

"Tom Sanders," Jenna says, "there is no way you are strong enough to—"

Tom may be the smallest boy in our class, but he sure can shove hard. His hands barrel into my back and I lunge forward, eating braid. But not for long because right away we are zooming and Jenna's braids are flying. We zip past Rachel, who has only made it halfway down the hill so far. We sail past Jolene and Meeka, who are walking up the hill with their matching purple sleds. We hit a bump and snow flies up, stinging my cheeks. We hit a bigger bump and *we* fly up. All I can see is a blur of sky and sleds and snow. All I can hear is Jenna screaming one high note like the highest key on my mom's piano.

We hit the hill hard and I howl. Jenna screams even higher and I feel her wiggle one boot off the toboggan. She digs it into the snow, but we don't slow down. We just do a sharp turn and a moment later we are tumbling down the hill, boots, braids, toboggan, and all.

When we finally stop, I untangle my legs from Jenna's arms and sit up. "Well," I say. "That was fun."

"Uh-huh," Jenna replies. She's lying flat on her back like a snow angel. Her eyes are wide open like maybe she's looking right into heaven.

"I guess Tom Sanders is stronger than you thought," I say.

"Uh-huh," Jenna says again.

Rachel waddles up to us and studies her sister. "Is she dead?"

Jenna gives Rachel a squint. "Of course not," she says, sitting up. "I'm not a baby like you."

"I'm not a baby," Rachel says. "I'm five and a half."

"Then why do you still wear diapers?"

Rachel punches her fists into her hips. "Pull-ups are not diapers. Mommy said so. And I only wear them at night. So there."

"So *what*," Jenna says, standing up and brushing off her snow pants. "You're going to have to stop wearing them when the *new* bay—"

Jenna bites back her words. She gets busy brushing her snow pants again.

"New what?" Rachel asks.

"New nothing," Jenna replies. Then she shoves the toboggan toward us with her boot. "You two take it. I'm bored of this little hill."

We watch Jenna walk away.

I look at Rachel. "I guess it's just you and me," I say.

"Good," she says back.

Dear Stella,

    I went sledding all afternoon. Then I came home and built a snowman with braces for my dad. When my neighbor Mr. Juhl saw it he told me I could build a snow toilet in his yard next. Mr. Juhl is a plumber. I said, "Maybe tomorrow," because I already had so much snow up my sleeves and down my pants I felt like an inside-out snowman. I even got snow in my underwear. Don't tell.

We didn't have school today, but I learned some stuff anyway.

For example, it's not a good idea to monkey pile more than four kids on a sled if you want to make it down the hill. Also, don't be the bottom monkey if you want to make it down alive.

Boys can scream just as loud as girls.

Dominic's old piece of cardboard works as good as Jenna's new toboggan.

Speaking of Jenna (the Screamer), I think she's more brave on the outside than she is on the inside.

I think I might be the other way around.

I also think Jenna is keeping a secret because twice she had to snap her mouth shut to keep something from slipping out, and I don't think it was gum. Once when she was arguing with Rachel, and once when Jolene told us she got a baby lizard for Christmas.

Maybe Jenna is getting a baby lizard too?

I get to see Stacey TOMORROW! I can't wait. (Which is no secret.)

Bye,
Ida (the Brave)

Chapter
3

Just as I'm heading out to the bus on Thursday morning my mom calls to me from the kitchen. "Did you feed your fish?"

"I'll do it when I get home," I call.

"Have you checked the filter lately?"

"I've been really busy!" I yell back.

"Fish need food, Ida," Mom says, stepping into the front hallway where I'm trying to get the door open fast. "And you're supposed to check the tank filter for gunk once a week."

I pull off a glove and grip the doorknob. "I know," I say. "But if I don't leave right now I'll miss the bus. And if I miss the bus, you'll have to drive me. And if you drive me, you'll make me feed my fish *and* clean the filter before we go and then I won't have any time before school to talk to Stacey."

Mom crosses her arms. "How would you feel if I sent you off to school with no breakfast, hmm?"

"Mom, swimming around a tiny little tank all day doesn't give you much of an appetite."

"Oh, really?" she says. "When was the last time you swam around a tank all day? Or sucked gunk through your gills?"

I try to come up with a good answer, one that will get me out the door extra fast, but before I do, Mom sighs. "Never mind. I'll feed your fish for you this one time. But you check the filter as soon as you get home. Got it?"

"Got it," I say. "Thanks." I turn the knob and head out the door.

"By the way," Mom calls as I clunk across the porch. "Did you name the fish yet?"

"Not yet," I call back as I hurry down the walk. "But I'm working on it!"

When I get to the bus stop, Quinn is trying to wrestle himself off the top of a snowbank. "Take that!" he yells, kickboxing the empty air. He follows up with a few rapid-fire karate chops, sound effects included. Quinn is not the biggest kid in our class, but he is fast. Not as fast as Randi Peterson, but still, pretty fast.

Ice beads dangle from Quinn's hat. He plants his lightning bolt gloves on his hips and says, "Had enough?" to nobody. A second later his arm whips behind his back. "Arrrrgggghhhh!"

Quinn's feet fly out from under him and he log rolls to the sidewalk. He lays at my feet, fake dead.

"Hi, Quinn," I say. "Um . . . what are you doing?"

Quinn squints an eye at me. "Warming up," he says. "For recess."

There are always snowbanks on our playground in winter because a plow comes through and piles it up around our big square of blacktop. Everyone plays king of the mountain on the banks, even though we're not supposed to push and shove at school.

Quinn jumps up and scrambles to the top of the bank again, grunting and beating his chest like he's the head snow monkey.

I keep walking.

Quinn's little sister, Tess, and Rachel Drews

waddle past me, following a connect-the-dots squirrel path in the snow.

Jenna is keeping watch for the bus. A toy alligator is keeping her company. It's almost as big as she is. She's squeezing it around the middle so tight, I'm surprised stuffing isn't oozing out of its red felt mouth.

I study the alligator's fat fuzzy body and glassy green eyes. "Planning to do a little wrestling at school?" I ask Jenna.

Jenna gives me a squint. "Ha, ha," she says. "It's Rachel's. She *had* to bring it for show-and-tell. My mom was feeling sick, so I'm stuck hauling it to her classroom."

"Your mom is sick?" I ask.

"Just temporarily," Jenna replies. "And just in the morning. She'll feel better this afternoon."

"Well, it's nice of you to help her," I say.

"I'm not doing it to be nice," Jenna says. "I'm doing it because I have to." She puckers her mouth like a raisin. "Jenna," she says in a fake-mom voice. "In this family we support and encourage each other. Now pick up that alligator and get to school!"

Jenna huffs and squeezes the alligator tighter. "My mom can be such a boss."

A minute later, the school bus comes around the corner and we all climb on.

When we get to school, Jenna, Rachel, Tess, and the alligator head to the kindergarten wing. Quinn zooms past me, catching up to Zane and Rusty. Zane has his arm in a cast.

"What happened to you?" I overhear Quinn ask Zane.

"Went sledding on Ricochet Ridge," Zane replies.

"Whoa . . ." Quinn says. "What did you do? Hit a tree?"

"Nah," Zane says. "Rusty dared me to go down standing up."

Rusty bobs his head.

"I would've made it too," Zane continues, "if some little kid hadn't been poking along in front of me."

"Yeah," Rusty says. "Zaney did a backside one eighty right over the kid! I swear he was airborne for five, ten seconds before he hit the hill."

"Snap, crackle, pop," Zane says. "Busted my arm in three places."

"*Cool*," Quinn says.

I hurry past the boys and head for the fourth-grade wing. I want to see Stacey before the bell rings.

As soon as I get there I notice the floor is as shiny as it was on the first day of school. Mr. Benson, our custodian, must have spent his holiday break scrubbing and waxing.

When I get to our coatroom, I hang up my jacket, kick off my boots, and slip on my sneakers. Then I pull my new box of oil pastels out of my backpack and go out to the hallway to find Stacey. But Randi Peterson finds me first.

Randi holds a bright orange basketball up to my nose. "Smell it," she says.

I take a sniff. "Smells like you got a new basketball for Christmas," I say.

Randi nods and presses her nose against it. She closes her eyes and breathes in. "*Ahhhh . . .*" she says. "There's nothin' like the smell of a new basketball." Then she opens her eyes. "I'm gonna baby it too. So it'll smell longer."

"Good plan," I say. "Did you get anything else?"

"The usual," Randi says, bouncing the ball on the shiny floor. "Books from my grandma. Clothes from my mom and dad. Video games from my brothers so they can play with them. Stuff like that. How about you?"

"I got *this*," I say, holding up my box of oil pastels.

"Crayons?" Randi says.

"Not *crayons*," I reply. "*Oil pastels*. Like real artists use." I turn the box over and show her the picture of *Arielle LaFayette, Award-Winning Artist*.

Randi studies the picture for a moment. "That's all you got?" she asks.

I fidget a little. "Well, no, but this is the *best* I got."

"Huh," she says, and sniffs her basketball.

Just then, I see Stacey walking toward us. I smile and wave, but she doesn't wave back because she's busy unzipping her shiny silver jacket and talking to Brooke.

It's no fun waving to someone who isn't waving back, so I pull my hand down and swallow my smile.

Stacey takes off her fuzzy purple earmuffs. They must be new, because I've never seen them before. Stacey looks kind of new too. Different. Her hair is pulled up into a high ponytail, which makes her look even taller than she did the last time I saw her, ten days ago. Plus, she's wearing a new outfit. It's the matching kind you see in girls' magazines. Red jumper. Blue turtleneck. Striped tights. White boots with furry trim and jingle bells at the ends of the laces.

Brooke has her long, dark hair pulled up into a high ponytail too. Only it's a lot curlier than usual. Like her head grew springs. It matches Stacey's ponytail perfectly and for one tiny second I wonder if they planned it.

I fiddle with the edge of my same old sweatshirt and squeak the toe of my same old sneaker against the floor. I got new clothes for Christmas too. Stuff from the Mish Mosh, which is my favorite store at the mall. Skinny jeans and two sweaters. Bright red baby-doll shirt and a matching bag. But I was so excited to see Stacey and to show her my oil pastels, I forgot to wear any of it.

Stacey jingles up to me and Randi. "Hi, you guys!" she says. She gives my arm a friendly squeeze.

"Hi!" I say back. "I like your new clothes."

"Thanks!" Stacey replies. "They're from my dad." She does a little step-turn like a model on a runway.

Brooke applauds.

"Cute," I say, doing my best grin. "When my dad picks out clothes for me I usually only wear them for pajamas."

Stacey giggles. "I think my dad's girlfriend helped him. Normally anything he buys me is too boyish."

"Ugh," Brooke says.

"What's wrong with boyish?" Randi asks, sniffing her basketball.

"Nothing," Brooke says, rolling her eyes.

I study Brooke's curly ponytail for a moment. "Did you get a perm or something?" I ask.

Brooke reaches up and unclips the springy curls from her regular hair. "Jade gave it to me," she says, jiggling the ponytail. Jade is Brooke's older sister. She knows a lot about hair and clothes because she's in high school. "See?" she says. "It's faux."

"*Fur?*" Randi says.

"Not *fur*," Brooke says back. "*Faux.* You know. Fake hair?"

"Are you sure?" Randi asks, giving the ponytail a poke. "Because I saw a dead squirrel on the way to school that looked a lot like that."

Brooke huffs and clips the ponytail back to her head.

Randi grins and bumps the basketball against her chin.

Just then Meeka and Jolene arrive. They take a quick tour of Brooke's new ponytail and Stacey's new clothes. Then they do the step-turn thing to show us *their* new outfits.

I brush my bangs over my paintbrush barrettes and slide my oil pastels into my back pocket.

"Jade also gave me *this,*" Brooke says, pulling a see-through plastic case out of her backpack. Six squares of eye shadow are lined up under the lid like little pads of butter. Light blue, bright blue. Light green, bright green. Light purple, bright purple. All glittery.

Brooke opens the lid and takes out a little

sponge-tipped stick. "The applicator has two ends, one for dark colors and one for light," Brooke tells us, all professional. She rubs one of the sponge ends across the bright purple pad. Then she looks at herself in the little built-in mirror while she glides the color across her left eyelid. Then she does her right eyelid. "Now for light purple under my eyebrows." Pretty soon her eyelids are very purple and glittery.

Brooke blinks at us.

Stacey squeals.

So do Meeka and Jolene.

Randi grunts.

"My mom won't let me wear makeup yet," Jolene says.

"Mine either," Meeka adds.

"Well," Brooke says, "I'm *really* only allowed to wear it for dance recitals and stuff, but that is just so unfair. I mean, I am *ten* now." She flutters her purple lids.

"I'm *almost* ten," Meeka says. "Let me try."

"Me too," Jolene adds, reaching for the sponge stick.

Brooke pulls back. "Everyone will get a turn," she

says. She looks the group over. "You first, Meeka."

Meeka does an excited little jump, lifts her chin, and closes her eyes.

Brooke makes a bright blue trail of eye shadow across Meeka's lids. "Jade says blue makes your eyes look bigger," Brooke informs us.

"What's wrong with the size of Meeka's eyes?" Randi asks.

"Nothing," Brooke replies. "But Jade says it's important to enhance what you have."

Brooke adds another layer of blue to Meeka. She lets the sponge slip past the corners of Meeka's eyes and swoop up like bird wings.

"There," Brooke says, holding the little mirror up to Meeka. "Now your eyes are really noticeable."

"Yep," I say.

Brooke glances at me. "Okay, Ida, you're next."

"Me? But I didn't say I wanted to—"

Brooke loads the sponge stick with bright green shadow. "Close your eyes," she says.

I close my eyes.

I can feel the sponge enhancing my eyelids all over the place. A minute later, Brooke steps back. "There," she says.

I blink my eyes open and see Stacey. "How do I look?"

"Good!" she says.

"*Better* than good," Brooke replies, holding the little mirror up to my eyes.

I see lots of green glitter where my plain eyelids used to be.

Randi frowns. "You look stup—"

"Great!" Stacey interrupts.

"Older," Meeka adds.

Jolene nods. "At least eleven."

I smile and look at my reflection in the mirror again. I do look older. Even taller. Maybe even prettier.

"Except for one thing," Brooke says.

"What?" I ask.

"Your eyes are perfect, but the rest of you is too . . . I don't know . . . plain."

"What's wrong with being plain?" Randi asks.

Brooke gives Randi a glance. "Nothing," she says. "Unless you count everything." She studies me again. Then her eyes brighten. "I know what's missing," she says. "Earrings!" Brooke gives her sparkly earlobe a flick. "You need glittery earrings to match your glittery eyes!"

"But I don't have pierced ears," I say.

"Well, what are you waiting for?" Brooke asks. "I've had my ears pierced since I was *three*."

"Don't listen to her, Ida," Randi says, poking a thumb at Brooke. "She's got too many holes in her head."

I glance at Randi's ears. They are bare. But all the other girls' earlobes glitter with earrings. The kind of earrings I would be wearing if my parents would let me. And if I wasn't afraid of getting poked.

Brooke gives Randi a squint and then gets busy with Jolene's eyelids. "All I'm saying is that Ida would look better with earrings. But if she doesn't want pierced ears, that's her choice."

"Um . . . it's not that I don't want them, exactly," I say. "It's just that my parents won't let me." I leave out the part about not feeling very brave when it comes to sharp objects.

Brooke snorts. "All you have to do is make your parents feel bad about not giving you what your friends have. Jade taught me that ages ago."

Jenna walks up to us just as Brooke finishes with Jolene.

"Purple, please," Stacey says, stepping up to Brooke and closing her eyes.

"Copycat," Brooke says, all teasey. She flutters her purple eyelids and giggles. Stacey giggles back. Then Brooke rubs the sponge stick across the little pad of purple eye shadow. Pretty soon Stacey's eyes match Brooke's eyes perfectly.

"What's going on?" Jenna asks.

"Brooke got eye shadow for Christmas," I explain.

Jenna studies all of our glittery eyelids. Then she lifts her chin. "That's nothing," she says. "Wait until you see what *I* got."

"*You* got makeup?" Brooke says. "I didn't think your mom would let you wear anything that didn't come from an organic farm." Brooke gives Jenna a tilted smile. "In fact, the last time I was at your house she wouldn't even let us paint our nails. She said the fumes might cause brain damage. Ha."

Jenna crosses her arms and squints. "Ancient history," she says. "See?"

42

Jenna holds up her hands. Each fingernail is painted bright orange.

"Um, hello?" Brooke says back. "It was right before Thanksgiving. I remember because your mom was making a tofu turkey. She spazzed when she smelled the polish and chased us out of the kitchen. Then she opened all the windows even though it was at least below zero outside."

"She was just worried about the fumes hurting the bay—the . . . the tofu turkey," Jenna says.

"Ew," Stacey says. "Tofu turkey sounds kind of gross. Did you actually eat it?"

"Well, duh, of course," Jenna says. "We eat it all the time. Too much animal protein makes you moody."

Brooke snorts. "That explains why you never are."

Brooke doesn't say it like a compliment. She says it in a mean way. A *not* best friend way.

"So what did *you* get for Christmas?" Jolene asks, blinking her bright blue eyelids at Jenna.

"I bet I know," I say to Jenna. "Your new toboggan, right?"

Jenna shakes her head. "Even better than that.

You'll see." She turns to the others. "You all will."

"When?" we ask.

Jenna squints at Brooke. "When I decide to bring it."

Brooke rolls her eyes.

Jenna does a step-turn and marches into class.

Chapter

4

It takes me longer than usual to find my desk, partly because I'm trying to blink very slowly so I won't smudge my eyelids and partly because Mr. Crow has rearranged our desks again. He likes to change things around so we don't get too bored with school.

Today the desks are in one big square all facing the center of the room. A bright rug covers the middle of the floor. It's got lots of different shapes woven into it. Rectangles. Circles. Triangles. Squares. Like if you looked into a giant kaleidoscope, the rug is what you would see.

A small table sits at the center of the rug. It has white cardboard shapes on it. Cube. Cylinder. Pyramid. Cone. I know that's what they are because I have a drawing book at home that talks about them.

All of our desks have name tags. The tags are different shapes too. Mine is a circle. Tom is sitting on my left. Quinn is on my right. I'm in the middle of a boy sandwich.

I look across the room and see Stacey Merriweather. I give her an *I-wish-I-could-sit-by-you* look and she gives me one back.

Mr. Crow steps into the center of our desk square. "Welcome back to class!" he says.

Nobody exactly cheers, even though we like Mr. Crow a lot.

"I hope you had a nice break," he continues, "and that you're ready for a great winter quarter."

Nobody exactly cheers again.

"What's with all the shapes?" Joey Carpenter asks, pointing to the little table.

Mr. Crow picks up the cardboard cube. "I'm glad you asked," he says. "We're starting a new math unit today and so I wanted to get us in *shape* right away." Mr. Crow does a little chuckle.

We all wait for more information.

Mr. Crow walks over to a new poster that's hanging on the wall. It has lots of geometric shapes on it. He points to each shape and we read off their names.

"Square!

"Oval!

"Pentagon!

"Hexagon!

"Octagon!

"Cylinder!"

"Good job!" Mr. Crow says after we finish doing the whole chart. "Now let's see how many of these shapes we can find in our classroom."

Mr. Crow gets Dominic and one of the Dylans to hand out worksheets that have *Shapes Hunt* printed across the top. All the shapes that are on the chart are on the worksheet.

"Get with a partner and hunt for each shape," Mr. Crow says. "For example, our chalkboard is shaped like a rectangle, so you can write *chalkboard* next to the rectangle shape on your worksheet. Some shapes will be easier to find than others, so look carefully and think creatively!"

Thinking creatively is one of Mr. Crow's favorite things to make us do.

Mr. Crow lets us pick our own partners, so of

course me and Stacey pick each other. I'm glad, because we don't have an even number of girls in our class. One girl always gets stuck being the leftover. Mr. Crow makes her join one of the pairs, unless he forgets. Then she either has to find a pair on her own or just pretend she has a partner and do the worksheet by herself.

Until Stacey started being my best friend, I got to be the leftover a lot.

Everyone starts seeing the easy shapes right away. Square floor tiles. Rectangle windows. The world globe for a sphere. But we're stuck on the harder shapes, like pentagon and hexagon.

Then Jolene says, "Hey, what about snow-flakes?" She points out the window at the falling snow. "Aren't they hexagons?" Jolene is good at shapes and math.

"That's right," Mr. Crow says. "All snowflakes have six sides, so they are all hexagons."

"Only no two snowflakes are exactly alike," Tom adds. Tom is good at answering questions no one even asked.

"Right again," Mr. Crow replies.

"They can't *all* be different," Jenna says.

"Um . . . y-yes they can," Tom replies. He's not so good at telling Jenna she's wrong. "They all have six sides, but they come in lots of different designs."

"An infinite number," Mr. Crow adds. "Just like people."

"Still," Jenna says, tapping her pencil against the edge of her clipboard. Jenna likes to work on a hard surface. "Snowflakes aren't *inside* our classroom, so they shouldn't count."

Mr. Crow smiles. "I'll make an exception for snowflakes," he says.

Everyone writes *snowflakes* by the hexagon shape. Then we get busy looking for pentagons.

Pretty soon I realize the more you look, the more shapes you see. Our wastebasket looks like an upside-down cone. Mceka's headband has diamond-shaped rhinestones. When Joey crawls across the floor to get Zane his dropped eraser, the treads on the bottom of his shoes look like octagons. And Zane's eraser is shaped like an oval. Mr. Crow's glasses are shaped like squares. Dominic's are circles. When Mr. Benson walks past our classroom doorway, I see the mop bucket he's pushing looks like a yellow cube.

It isn't until Jenna makes a big deal about Mr. Crow's teacup being a cylinder that I notice something else.

Mr. Crow forgot about the leftover girl today.

I know because I see Jenna write *teacup* next to the cylinder on her worksheet. Only nobody else is writing it with her.

"Jenna," I whisper. "You can be with me and Stacey if you want."

Stacey looks up from her worksheet. "Sure, Jenna, you can be with us."

"Oh, isn't that sweet?" Brooke says as she and Randi walk by. "Stacey and Ida are taking in a stray puppy." She gives Jenna a smirk.

Jenna gives her one back.

"What's with you two lately?" Randi asks, looking at Brooke and Jenna. "It's like the Ice Capades around here."

Brooke's face goes all innocent.

Jenna just goes. To the other side of the room.

Dear Stella,
    Today I learned that all squares are

50

rectangles, but not all rectangles are squares. I'm still trying to wrap my brain around that one.

Brooke snuck eye shadow to school. I spent the whole day trying not to rub my eyelids, which used up a lot of my concentration. That's probably why I got four wrong on my social studies worksheet.

I wiped the eye shadow off before I got home. I don't think my mom and dad would be as excited about glittery eyelids as I am.

Everyone else wiped it off too. Except for Randi, because she wasn't wearing any. And Jenna, because she wasn't there when Brooke showed us how to put it on. But I don't think Jenna would have worn it anyway. Because of the mean way Brooke was talking to her. Like her words were covered in prickles.

Jenna has always been the boss of us, but now Brooke is acting like she got voted our new boss. Only Jenna didn't get to vote.

It reminds me of a nature show about wolves my dad and me watched a couple of weeks ago. One wolf was in charge of the pack, but then a

51

new wolf wanted to be the boss. So the new wolf kept nipping and nipping at the other wolf until it finally got tired of all that nipping and let the new wolf have its way.

I think Brooke wants to be in charge of us now.

And Jenna is getting nipped.

I set down my journal and slide off my bed. A long mirror hangs behind my door. I study my eyelids in it. Then I study the rest of me. I sigh because I look exactly like myself again.

My oil pastels are still in my backpack, so I dig them out and find the dark green stick.

I rub it across my eyelids and look at myself in the mirror again, tilting and blinking.

"You look at least eleven," I say to my reflection.

I catch a glimpse of George in the mirror. He's leaning against my fish tank, watching me.

"What do you think?" I ask him, blinking fast.

George glances away.

"Well, I like it," I say, closing my box of oil pastels.

I walk over to George and slide him aside. I look at my fish. "Hi . . . Elmo?"

My fish darts behind the dentures. The pirate lifts his jug.

"I guess that's not your name either," I say.

The water pump gurgles and I think about the filter inside. "Looks good to me."

I grab a tissue and wipe off my eyes.

Then I walk over to my bed and pick up my journal again.

Me and Stacey went to the Purdee Good after she got done with dance class today. We shared a giant cookie like always. Plus, we talked about what we did over our holiday break and all the prescuts we got and everything. I told Stacey all about my fish and she said I should name him Elmo. I told her I liked it, even though it sounded a little furry for a fish.

Then I finally showed Stacey my box of oil pastels. She loved them just like I hoped she would. Right away we started drawing pictures on paper place mats. Kelli was doing her waitress job and when she saw our drawings she said they were good enough to be in a museum. She made us autograph them and then she hung them up for everyone to see.

Then Stacey took out her ponytail because it was giving her a hairache. I let her wear my paintbrush barrettes and she let me try on her jingle bell boots.

They almost fit me.

Jenna has a big secret she's bringing to school tomorrow. She won't tell us what it is, even though she keeps reminding us how much we're going to love it.

We'll see.

Bye,
Ida

Chapter
5

Jenna doesn't say a word to me about her big secret at the bus stop on Friday morning, even though her lips look like they are starting to crack from keeping it in.

When we get to school, she won't tell anyone else either. Not until all seven of us arrive. We're still waiting for Randi.

Brooke gets out her eye shadow and hands it to me. "Chop, chop, Ida," she says. "Put some on and pass it around."

I do one of my eyelids blue and one of them purple. Stacey takes the sponge stick from me and does her eyes the same way.

"Wait," Brooke says, taking the eye shadow from us. "I have a better idea."

Brooke does three curved stripes across her

eyelids—purple, green, and blue. "Ha," she says. "I'm a rainbow."

Jolene and Meeka do rainbow eyes too.

Not Jenna, though. She keeps pacing back and forth, waiting for Randi.

When she finally arrives, Jenna opens her backpack and pulls out a square box. It's bright purple with lots of curly writing. I see four girls on the lid. They all look very excited to be there. Jenna quickly hides the box against her chest and I hear something rattle inside.

"What is it?" Stacey asks Jenna, passing the eye shadow to Randi.

"A game," Jenna says.

"Which game?" Randi asks. "Yahtzee? Twister? Trouble?"

Jenna shakes her head and licks her lips. "It's better than any of those."

"Well, which one then?" Brooke asks.

Jenna turns the box over so we can all read the name on the lid.

"Truth or dare!" we all say together.

"I *love* truth or dare!" Jolene says.

"Me too!" Meeka adds. "My sister has the electronic version."

"*Electronic* version?" Randi says. She passes the eye shadow to Brooke without putting any on. "Me and my brothers just dare each other to put ketchup on our ice cream, or eat a dog biscuit, or lick the toilet." She gives her basketball a bounce. "No electricity required."

"Well, if you want to play *my* truth or dare game," Jenna says, "you have to roll the dice and choose a card." Jenna opens the game box and shows us a board with places where two stacks of cards go.

"How do you play?" I ask.

"See the dice?" Jenna says. "If you roll two T's you have to choose someone to take a truth card. Two D's and the person has to take a dare card. If you get a T and a D the person gets to choose—truth *or* dare. They have to do what the card says no matter what."

"Fun," I say.

"What do the cards tell you to do?" Stacey asks, nudging closer to Jenna.

Jenna puts the lid back on the box. "You'll see," she says. "At recess."

The bell rings and Jenna shoves the box inside her backpack. Everyone heads into the classroom, giggling and whispering about the game.

I follow along, blinking slowly and thinking about the secrets I might have to tell.

And the stuff I might have to lick.

Maybe Randi was right.

Maybe Jenna's game is *Trouble* after all.

When it's time for our first recess, Mr. Crow starts herding the boys to the coatroom. But we girls hang back. Jenna gets the truth or dare game out of her backpack and we all sit in a circle on the big shapes rug.

"What's that?" Quinn asks, taking a shortcut across the rug to get back to his desk. He grabs his sweatshirt off his chair and then pokes his head into our circle.

"Jenna got truth or dare for Christmas," Brooke explains.

Quinn studies the cards Jenna is sorting into two piles. "Lemme see," he says, snatching a truth card from Jenna.

"Hey!" Jenna shouts, giving Quinn's hand a slap.

"Ouch!" Quinn pulls his hand away and steps back, reading the card he swiped. *"Do you still suck your thumb?"*

Quinn grins and looks at Jenna. "Well? Do you?"

I gulp a little because sometimes when I wake up at night my thumb is in my mouth. I have no idea how it got there. I would mostly die if I had to tell the other girls that secret.

Plus, if I got a card that said *Do you still play with baby toys?* I would mostly die again because the answer is *yes*. I have a toy farm set I keep under my bed. I got it from Grandma May when I was even littler than Rachel. Sometimes I pull it out and play with the plastic animals, especially the pink cow and the red horse. They always end up getting married. And the orange rooster who tries to run down the other animals with the toy tractor. Sometimes my Barbies get involved too. It's a lot of fun to play farm, but I have to be careful because the barn door moos when you open and close it. Noisy secrets are hard to keep.

Jenna jumps up and grabs for the card.

Quinn butt-slides across his desk to get away. "So, is that a *yes?*" he says to her.

"I do *not* suck my thumb," Jenna snaps. "And you are not allowed to play!" She reaches across Quinn's desk and grabs his wrist.

Quinn squirms away and wipes his arm on his jeans. "Yuck!" he says. "Your thumb's wet. Have you been sucking it?"

We all giggle.

Jenna growls.

"All right, all right," Mr. Crow says, coming back into the room. "What's going on?"

"Quinn stole my card!" Jenna shouts.

Mr. Crow looks at Quinn. "Did you?"

Quinn shrugs. "I was just having a little fun." He flicks the card at Jenna. It flutters to the floor.

Jenna snatches it up and sits back down.

"Head outside," Mr. Crow says. "All of you."

"But we're playing a game!" Jenna says.

Mr. Crow shakes his head. "Save it for later." He steers Quinn toward the coatroom. "You could all use some fresh air."

Jenna gives Quinn a glare.

Quinn flashes another grin and darts out the door.

Jenna throws the game back into its box. "It's too windy to take this outside," she grumbles. "The cards might blow away."

"If we eat lunch quick, maybe Mr. Crow will let us come back to the room early and play then," Stacey suggests.

We all agree and head for the coatroom. We put on our stuff and tromp outside.

A few kids are shooting baskets on the blacktop. Other kids are playing football in the snow. But most kids are climbing around on the big snowbanks that circle the blacktop like a ring of miniature mountains.

"Hey, look," Randi says, pointing to one of the snowbanks. All of the boys from our class are crawling up and down it. Except for Zane. He's standing at the bottom of the bank, shouting directions as the other boys pack and chisel the snow into a fort.

Randi turns to us. "Let's build a fort too. Then we can bomb the boys!" She scoops up some snow from the edge of the blacktop and lets it fly. It just misses Zane's head.

Zane whips around. "No fair!" he shouts at Randi. "I'm broken!" He flaps the loose sleeve of his jacket where his left arm would be if it wasn't in a cast.

"You only need one hand to throw a snow-ball," Randi shouts back and lets another one fly.

"But it takes two hands to pack one!" Zane starts scrambling up the side of the boys' snow-bank.

Quinn's head pops up from behind it. He sees Jenna and cracks a smile. "Hey, baby-Jenna!" he shouts. "Waa, waa, waa-aaa . . ." Then he sticks his thumb into his mouth and pretends to suck it.

Jenna scowls at Quinn. Then she marches toward a snowbank that's kitty-corner from the boys' fort. "C'mon!" she shouts to us. "Let's get 'em!"

We hurry after her. A minute later we are packing the top of our bank into a wall, carving out peepholes, and making ammunition.

The boys must figure out that we're up to some-thing, because pretty soon I see Quinn sneaking toward us.

I stop packing snowballs and give Randi a nudge. "I spy a spy," I say, pointing to Quinn.

Randi looks up and sees Quinn sneak-crouching toward our fort. Her eyes narrow and the corners of her mouth curl up. She wipes the back of her mitten across her nose and says, "We've got company, men." She calls us men even though it's obvious we are girls.

Everyone peeks over the top of our snowbank.

Quinn sees us and grabs a second grader for camouflage.

The bell rings and the blacktop starts to clear. Quinn's second grader squirms away.

"Ready . . . aim . . . fire!" Randi shouts. Even though I can't throw very far, I can throw straight. My snowball catches Quinn square in the chin.

He spits snow, then he smiles. "Killer shot, Ida!"

Even though he's the enemy, I smile back.

Quinn's a goner. Before he knows it, Jenna's gotten him in the gut, Jolene's slammed his right shoulder, and Meeka his left.

He turns and scrambles back to his fort, taking three more shots in the back from Randi, Stacey, and Brooke. The other boys haul him over the top of the snowbank.

The playground attendant blows her whistle. "Head inside!" she shouts at us.

The boys take off.

But not us girls.

We stand on top of our snowbank, cheering and beating our chests like we are the bravest girls in the world.

I just hope I'm brave enough for truth or dare.

Chapter

6

Just like we hoped, Mr. Crow lets us come back to our classroom early after lunch. Jenna takes out the truth or dare game again and sets it on the shapes rug. We all huddle up.

"I'll start," Jenna says, rolling the dice. "See? I rolled a T and a D. That means I get to pick someone to do a truth card *or* a dare card. It's up to me. Any questions?"

"Yeah," Brooke says. "How come you get to go first?"

"Because it's my game," Jenna says. "If you don't like it, you can go throw snowballs at the boys."

"Hmm," Brooke says. "Tempting."

Jenna looks us over like she's a spider and we're a bunch of flies caught in her web. "I choose Stacey," she says. "Truth or dare?"

Stacey wiggles closer to me. "Which one should I choose?" she whispers.

"Definitely dare," I whisper back.

"Really?" Stacey says. "Why?"

"If you do a dare you will only feel silly for a minute. But if you have to tell the truth about some big secret, you might feel silly forever."

"*Choose*, Stacey," Jenna says impatiently. "Truth or dare?"

Stacey thinks for a moment. *"Dare,"* she says, smiling at me.

Stacey draws a dare card and reads it out loud. *"Dance like a chicken and snort like a pig!"*

Everyone squeals.

Stacey jumps up and starts flapping and snorting. It would take a lot more than a chicken dance to embarrass her.

We all laugh like crazy.

Stacey takes a bow.

"Now you roll the dice," Jenna tells Stacey.

Stacey does and two T's land faceup. Someone has to tell the truth.

Stacey's eyes wander from girl to girl. They land on me. "Ida," she says. "I choose you."

"Gee, thanks," I say.

I draw a truth card from the stack. *"Tell about the grossest thing you've ever done."*

Randi snorts. "I could come up with a million."

I think for a moment. "Once, I sucked all the salt off a bag of corn chips."

"What's so gross about that?" Jenna asks.

"Afterward, I put the chips back in the bag."

"Eew!" Brooke says.

"Then later," I add, "my dad ate them."

"Double *eew*!" Jolene says.

"Did you tell your dad?" Meeka asks.

"Um . . . I told him 'No thanks' when he asked if I wanted any."

Everyone laughs.

Randi gives me a thumbs-up.

I smile a little because having to tell a silly story isn't as bad as having to dance like a chicken.

It's my turn. I roll a T and a D.

"You have to choose someone who hasn't had a turn yet," Jenna informs me.

"Uh-huh," I say. "Thanks for the tip."

Jenna sits up higher on her knees. She flicks her braids off her shoulders and does a cough.

I glance around the circle. "I choose . . .
Meeka," I say.

Meeka smiles.

Jenna slouches.

Meeka picks up a truth card. *"What do you
want to be when you grow up?"* she reads from the
card.

"Lame," Randi mumbles.

"That's easy," Meeka says. "I want to be a doctor, like my mom."

"Eew," Brooke says. "Too much blood."

"And guts," Randi adds. "Once, my brother cut
his hand so bad the *meat* was hanging out."

Brooke plugs her ears. "I don't want to know."

"It was all pink and bumpy," Randi continues.
"Like that fungus that grows on tree stumps."

Brooke rocks and hums.

Randi shakes her head. "Man, you should
have seen the doctor try to fit it all back inside his
hand."

The rest of us plug our ears too.

Except for Meeka. She just smiles and rolls the
dice.

Chapter

7

It was too cold to go sledding over the weekend, so I mostly just read and watched TV and worked on fish names. I made a whole list of names, but I didn't like any of them, so I used my oil pastels to draw a picture of my fish over the list. Now I have a very colorful fish with lots of names hidden inside.

"Did you feed your fish?" Mom asks as she pulls my jacket hood up over my hat on Monday morning. She winds a long scarf around my neck and ties a knot to keep out the cold.

"Yep," I say. "Yesterday."

Mom frowns. "Ida, you're supposed to feed him . . . her . . . *it* . . . every morning." I slip the knot up over my mouth.

"What about the filter? Did you check it for gunk?"

"I'm pretty sure it's gunk-free," I say through my knot. "I have a very clean fish."

Mom narrows her eyes. "After school," she says, "feed that no-name fish and check the filter."

I nod and pull on my gloves. "A little help with the door, please?"

Mom pulls open the front door. Icy air sweeps in.

Mom shivers. "Maybe I should drive you."

I slip on my backpack and slide past her. "I'm already bundled," I say. "Hardly any air is getting through."

I step onto the porch and Mom closes the door. My nose hairs stand at attention in the cold air. I pull down my scarf knot so I can puff out a few breath-signals. Then I squeak down the sidewalk pretending I'm Laura Ingalls walking across a frozen prairie.

Two settlers appear on the horizon.

Jenna and Rachel.

They get to the bus stop at the same time I do. Quinn and Tess aren't around. They must have gotten a ride.

"I brought it again," Jenna says, shifting her

eyes toward the truth or dare box she's got tucked under her arm. "If you sit by me—"

"Hey!" Rachel interrupts. "I'm not zipped!"

Jenna glances at Rachel's unzipped coat. "So, zip it!" she says.

"Mommy always does it for me," Rachel says back. Her chin starts to quiver and her eyes shut tight. "I'm getting froze!"

"Don't be a crybaby," Jenna says, setting the truth or dare box on the sidewalk. "Your eyes will freeze shut." She grabs the tab on Rachel's zipper and gives it a quick tug.

"Not so fast, or you'll zip my chin!" Rachel says. "Mommy never zips my chin."

"Then keep your chin up," Jenna says.

Rachel lifts her chin.

Jenna yanks the zipper.

When the bus comes around the corner, Jenna grabs the game box and turns to me. "If you sit by me on the bus," she says, "we can play on our way to school."

I don't usually sit with Jenna on the bus. She's not any bigger than me, but she's the kind of person that takes up a lot of room.

Still, she did ask nicely, so I say okay.

Jenna steers Rachel into one of the front seats and then follows me to a back seat.

We sit down, loosen our scarves, and pull off our gloves. Jenna takes a stack of cards out of the game box. "We don't have much time," she says as the bus starts to move forward. "Let's just do some of the truth cards."

"Okay," I say.

"And here's a rule," she adds. "We *both* have to answer each card."

I shrug. "Okay again."

She does a quick nod. "I'll go first."

Jenna draws a card and reads it out loud. *"What's your dream vacation?"* She looks up, thinking. "My dream vacation is camping at a state park."

"But your family goes camping at a state park *every* summer," I say. "It can't be a dream vacation if you go there all the time."

"Why not?" Jenna asks.

"Because you have to go somewhere . . . *dreamy*. Somewhere that starts with a letter at the end of the alphabet. Like Quebec or Venezuela or Utah. Not a plain old state park."

Jenna thinks again. "Okay, how about this," she says. "My dream vacation is to go camping at Yosemite. That's a *national* park and it starts with a Y."

I nod. "Better."

"Now you answer," Jenna says. "What's your dream vacation?"

I rub my nose, thinking. "Maybe New Zealand," I say. "It has a Z, plus I think it's already tomorrow there. If I leave right now, I can skip a whole day of school."

I do a clever smile.

Jenna does a squint. "Skipping school will get you sent to the principal's office. You should pick a place that's closer. That just makes sense."

"It's a *dream* vacation, Jenna," I say. "Dreams aren't supposed to make sense."

The bus slows to a stop and more kids pile on. I take a new card from the stack. *Who is your best friend?* I laugh. "That's easy. Stacey Merriweather."

Jenna's mouth does a twitch. "Of course," she says. She snatches the card from me and puts it at the bottom of the stack. "My turn." She draws a card from the top.

"Wait," I say. "You have to answer the question too, remember? Who's *your* best friend?"

I know Jenna will say Brooke, even though they've been fighting lately. They've been best friends forever.

Jenna does the twitch again. "I changed my mind," she says. "We don't have time to *both* answer."

"But you said—"

Jenna quickly reads her card out loud. *"What is your worst bad habit?"* She thinks for a moment. "I bite my nails," she says. "What's yours?"

I roll my eyes. "You just said we don't have time to *both* answer every card."

Jenna shrugs. "I changed my mind again."

"You *can't* keep changing the rules, Jenna. Either we both answer *every* card or we *don't*!"

The bus hits a bump and everyone bounces in their seats. One kid bounces onto another kid's lap, just to get a laugh.

But me and Jenna sit stiff and still.

The bus pulls up to our school. I glance at Jenna. "Okay," I grumble. "My bad habit is I sing in the shower. Country."

The bus door opens and kids start piling off.

Jenna stands up, but she doesn't move. She just stays there, like a snowman starring straight ahead. "I don't have one," she finally says.

I groan. "But you just said your bad habit is biting your nails."

Jenna whips me a look. "I'm not answering *that* question, okay? I'm answering the one I skipped." She tosses the cards back into the box, grabs her stuff, and shoves down the aisle.

I sit there, confused.

Then I remember the question she skipped.

Who is your best friend?

When I get to our hallway I see the other girls are already there. So is Mr. Crow. He's talking to them, only they aren't talking back. They just nod and study their shoes. Mr. Crow walks away just as I catch up to Jenna.

"Mr. Crow told us we can't wear eye shadow in class anymore," Brooke tells us when Jenna asks them what was going on. She snaps her eye shadow case closed. "He says it's causing a distraction."

Brooke narrows her eyes at Randi. "This is all your fault."

"Huh?" Randi says.

Brooke pulls a little package of tissues from a pocket in her backpack and starts wiping purple eye shadow off her eyes. "If you hadn't put peanut butter on your eyelids in the lunchroom last Friday, Mrs. Kettleson wouldn't have come out to see what everyone was laughing about. And then she wouldn't have told on us to Mr. Crow. And *then* Mr. Crow wouldn't be inspecting eyelids this morning."

Randi shrugs. "I was just having a little fun," she says.

Brooke hands a tissue to Meeka. She pulls out two more and hands them to Stacey and Jolene.

Jenna crosses her arms and lifts her chin. "I told you wearing makeup at school would get you into trouble, Brooke. If you had just lis—"

"You are not the boss of me, Jenna Drews," Brooke interrupts.

Jenna's mouth snaps shut.

Everyone is quiet.

"Um . . . I was getting tired of glittery eyelids anyway," I say.

"I'm glad it's over too," Randi says. "You guys looked stupid."

"We did *not*," Brooke snaps.

Randi shrugs. "Whatever. Who wants to race me to the snow fort?"

Randi zips up her jacket and pulls on a face mask. "Anyone?" she says. "I'll give you a head start."

"Our lungs might freeze," Meeka says. "That's not healthy."

"Plus the bell is going to ring any minute," Jolene adds. "There's not enough time."

"I can run there and back ten times before the bell rings," Randi says. "C'mon, who's with me?"

I glance at Stacey to see if she wants to go. But Stacey is already heading into the classroom with Brooke and the others.

I turn to Randi. "I guess no one feels like racing today."

Randi shrugs. "No one feels like doing anything lately, except wearing stupid makeup and playing stupider games."

I shift a little in my shoes.

Randi pulls on her gloves and heads to the hallway. "Last chance," she says, looking back at me.

"Maybe next time," I say, and follow after the others.

When it's time for our morning recess, Ms. Stevens, our principal, tapes a sign to the playground door that says *INSIDE*. That means it's too cold to play outside today.

All the boys start a game of silent ball in our classroom. To play, you sit on top of your desk and toss a squishy ball around, only you can't talk and you can't get off your desk unless you miss the ball. Then you're out.

It's a fun game, but today all the girls head to the reading corner to play truth or dare. Jenna opens the game box and sets the board on the floor. We gather in a circle around it. I sit next to Jenna. Stacey sits next to me.

Jolene rolls the dice.

Two D's.

She chooses Brooke to take a dare card.

Brooke reads the card to herself. "Oh, no," she says.

"What do you have to do?" Stacey asks.

"Act like someone in your group," Brooke reads.

"Let everyone guess who you are pretending to be."

Brooke stands up. She thinks for a minute. Then she messes up her hair like she hasn't brushed it for a week. She pretends to bounce a basketball. "Dudes!" she shouts. "Who wants to get their pants beat off?"

Everyone laughs. "Randi!" we all shout. Brooke wipes her sleeve across her nose and says, "Yup."

We all laugh again. If Brooke was trying to get back at Randi for putting peanut butter on her eyelids, it didn't work. Even Randi is laughing.

Randi jumps up next to Brooke and takes a bow.

"Sit down, Randi," Jenna snaps. "It's not your turn."

All the laughter dribbles away. Randi stops bowing, but she doesn't sit down. She just grins and says, "Hey, who am *I* pretending to be?" She gives Brooke a fake scowl and shakes her finger. "Follow the rules or I'll break your neck!" She says it in a sharp voice. A Jenna voice.

Everyone starts laughing. But we suck it back in when Jenna jumps up.

"It's *not* your turn," Jenna says. "If you can't follow the rules, you can't play my game."

Randi snickers and sits down. "You win," she says. "I quit." She leans back on her elbows and stretches out her legs. "This game is for babies anyway. The cards don't make you do *real* dares."

"*Real* dares?" Stacey asks.

Randi nods. "You know, stuff like . . ." She looks up at the ceiling, thinking. Then her mouth curls up at the corners and she zeroes in on Jenna. "I *dare* you to tell Zane you *like* him."

Everyone gasps.

Then giggles.

Then gasps again.

"I *don't* like Zane," Jenna says.

"So?" Randi sits up. "I didn't dare you to *marry* him. Just *tell* him you like him. Or are you *chicken*?"

Red splotches appear on Jenna's neck and cheeks. "I am *not* chicken," she says.

Randi does her grin again. "Prove it."

Jenna glances at Zane. He's sitting on top of his desk, chewing on a pink eraser. Zane says chewing on an eraser makes his broken arm itch less. But Zane has been chewing on erasers since kindergarten.

Jenna glances back at us. Her eyes lock on mine. She doesn't say a word, but it feels like she's asking me a question.

What should I do?

"Um . . ." I start to say. But before I can say anything else, Jenna jerks away and walks toward Zane. The closer she gets to him, the slower she walks. Like her legs are freezing up.

Randi scoots onto her knees and nudges forward. "This is gonna be good," she whispers.

We all nudge forward too.

Zane doesn't notice Jenna at first. He's too busy chewing on his eraser and throwing the silent ball when it comes to him.

Jenna gives Zane's shoulder a poke. She has to poke it three times before he glances back.

"Wha?" Zane asks, shifting the eraser with his tongue.

Jenna doesn't answer. She doesn't even move. Except for her chin, which is quivering.

"I . . . I . . . like you," she says.

Zane shifts the eraser again. "Huh?"

Jenna's splotches get even redder. "Y-you heard me," she says. Then she whips around and marches back to us.

The silent ball bounces off Zane's head. He's out.

Jenna crumples next to me. She pulls her knees up to her chest, wraps her arms around them, and buries her face.

"Wow," I say. "That was really brave, Jenna."

Everyone agrees.

Randi grins. "Now that's what I call a *real* dare."

"Ooooo. . . ." Brooke says. "I just had the best idea!"

"What?" Meeka asks.

"Let's make up our *own* dares," Brooke says. "We can make each other do whatever we want!"

Everyone squirms and giggles.

I gulp.

Jenna doesn't say a word.

Dear Stella,
    Guess what? Jenna told me she doesn't have a best friend and I think she was being true.

Then Randi dared her to tell Zane she likes him, which is definitely not true. I don't know who she likes, but I'm positive it's not Zane. I mean, he chews erasers. No girl likes a boy who does that. Plus, she signed a piece of paper that said I DO NOT LIKE ZANE. She made Zane sign it too.

After Jenna showed us the paper, Stacey said if she liked a boy it would not be Zane. And then Brooke said who would it be? Stacey said maybe Dominic or probably Quinn. And then Brooke said probably Quinn for her too. Then they asked me who I would pick if I liked a boy and I said oops, look at the time. Then I ran out to the bus.

Brooke probably would have called me a copycat if I picked Quinn. Only not in a teasey-nice way like she does with Stacey.

But before any of that happened, Brooke decided we should make our own dare cards. So that's what I've been doing since I got home from school. Jolene donated some kitten note cards she had in her desk. We each got three. Here's what I wrote on mine:

* Tell Mr. Crow there is a spider in his hair.
* At lunch, eat the fruit cocktail.
* Touch Dylan Anderson's shoe.

Luckily, we made a rule that you can't choose your own card, so I won't get stuck doing any of mine, especially not the last one. Dylan lives on a farm, so there's always crusty stuff stuck to his shoes that looks like it might have once belonged to a cow.

I hope Stacey doesn't have to do my shoe dare. I would still be her best friend if she did, but I might make her wash her hands first.

And maybe I hope Jenna doesn't have to do it either. If you are short on best friends, the last thing you want to do is touch a crusty shoe.

Chapter

8

Jenna looks over my three dare cards the next morning while we wait for the bus.

But all she does is huff. Then she pulls three bent cards out of her coat pocket and hands them to me. This is what they say:

> This is stupid.
> This is stupid.
> This is stupid.

"Brooke won't like it," I say, handing the cards back to Jenna.

"So?" Jenna says.

"So, if you two are already fighting, this will just make it worse."

"We're beyond fighting," Jenna says.

"What happened?" I ask. "I mean, you and Brooke were always best friends and now you're acting like you're best enemies."

"Nothing happened," Jenna says. "I'm just tired of the way she always bosses everyone around."

Rachel walks up to me and taps my arm. "Don't forget," she says. "You got to walk me to your house after school." Rachel starts piano lessons with my mom today, so I have to walk her to my house and home afterward.

"I won't forget," I say.

Rachel turns to her sister. "See, Jenna?" she says. "Ida won't forget me."

Jenna rolls her eyes. "Drop it, Rachel."

Rachel turns back to me. "Jenna forgot me yesterday," she whispers. "She was supposed to come and get me from Tess's house when the little hand got to the five, but she didn't come and didn't come and I might have cried a little."

"Stop making such a big deal," Jenna says. "You got to eat supper there, didn't you?"

"Yes, but tacos don't taste so good when it's getting dark. And when nobody is keeping their promise to you." Rachel hiccups.

Jenna sighs. "I told you I was sorry. That's all I can do."

The bus rumbles toward us and we step up to the curb. Rachel taps my arm again. "You won't forget me, will you Ida?" she asks.

"Nope," I say. "I'll write myself a note as soon as I get to school and stick it to my desk. And if you see me in the hall today, you can remind me then too."

Rachel smiles.

Jenna huffs and climbs on the bus.

When all the girls get to school we huddle together in the hallway and take out the dare cards we made. Jenna doesn't exactly huddle. But she doesn't walk away either.

Brooke takes all the cards and shuffles them up.

"Okay," she says, fanning the cards like a magician. "Now we each choose a card and do what it says."

"What happens if we don't?" Meeka asks.

Brooke thinks for a moment. "Then you have to do something *doubly* bad."

"A double-dog dare!" Randi says. "Once I

double-dog dared my brother to yell *Fire!* when our dad was taking a nap."

"What happened?" Stacey asks.

"My dad shot out of his recliner like he was a human cannonball. Then my brother got grounded for a week." Randi laughs. "It was great."

"Did you get grounded too?" Stacey asks.

"Nope," Randi says. "My brother never spilled the beans. When you take a dare, you have to swear never to tell on the person who dared you."

"What happens if you do?" I ask.

Randi shakes her head slowly. "Then you're up for a *triple*-dog dare."

"Ooooo . . ." Brooke says. "I heard Jade and her friends talking about triple-dog dares once."

Jolene nods. "My brother got one last year."

"What did he have to do?" Stacey asks.

"He wouldn't tell," Jolene replies. "But he smelled so bad afterward my mom threw away his clothes. Then she shaved his head."

We all gulp and fiddle with our hair.

Brooke puts her hand into the center of our circle. "Don't spill the beans," she says, "or you get a triple-dog dare."

Everyone puts their hand on top of Brooke's. "Don't spill the beans," we all say together.

The bell rings and kids start heading into the classroom. Brooke holds the cards out to us again. "Choose," she says.

We each choose a card and head inside.

I'm just about to read my dare when Tom sits down next to me at his desk. "I brought that book I told you about," he says, sliding a big, thick book from his desk to mine.

"You told me about a book?" I ask, hiding my dare card in my hand.

"Um . . ." Tom says. "No. Not yet." He pauses to rub his eyebrow. "But you're such a good artist, I knew you'd like it." He nudges the book toward me.

There's a picture of a bald man on the cover. His eyes are shiny and round, like black buttons. He creeps me out a little. Like he can actually see me. Maybe even see *through* me. Still, something about him seems familiar.

"Who is he?" I ask Tom, pointing at the picture on the book cover.

"Pablo Picasso," Tom says. He flips open the book. "The famous artist."

"Hey, I've seen that sculpture," I say, pointing to a picture of a giant creature that looks sort of like a monkey. "My aunt Margo took me to Chicago once and it was there."

"Cool," Tom says. "I wish I could see some of Picasso's sculptures. He rules."

I turn a few pages and feel my stomach do a little jump. "We saw *that* painting in Chicago too!" I point to a picture of a man who is drawn in different shades of blue. He's hunched over a guitar like he's playing a sad song. "It was in a museum there. I remember because if you look carefully you can see another painting of a lady underneath." I show Tom the half-hidden lady in the picture.

"Maybe Picasso made a mistake, so he drew a new picture over the old one," Tom says.

I nod. "A do-over. Even artists get them."

"Or maybe he just thought the first picture was lame," I hear someone say.

I look up and see Quinn leaning in for a closer look at the book. He studies the picture of the blue man with the guitar. "How come he looks so bendy? Like his bones are made out of Silly Putty."

Tom laughs. "He's supposed to look that way. Picasso used lots of weird angles and shapes in his paintings. He was trying to show the way people *feel*, not the way they actually *look*."

"Well, this guy must *feel* sick," Quinn says, "because he *looks* like he needs major surgery." He leans back in his chair and burps.

Mr. Crow starts taking attendance and Tom puts the book inside his desk. "I've got more books about Picasso," Tom whispers to me. "If you want to see them sometime."

I shrug. "Okay."

Tom sits back, smiling. He closes his desk lid and rubs his eyebrow.

I unfold the dare card I have hidden in my hand and peek at it.

This is stupid.

I frown. Then I lean forward so I can see Jenna. She sits on the other side of Tom. I squint at her until she looks at me. I hold up the card.

"You have to give me a *real* dare," I whisper.

Jenna looks away.

I dig a pencil and a little cube of sticky notes out of my desk. First I write a note to remind me about my promise to Rachel. I stick it to my desk.

Then I write a note to Jenna.

If I don't do a real dare, everyone will call me chicken!

I fold the note and slide it onto Tom's desk. "Pass this to Jenna," I whisper.

A moment later Jenna picks up my note, reads it, and scribbles an answer. Tom slides it back to me.

Then I dare you to let them call you chicken.

I sit back and sigh.

When Mr. Crow goes next door to borrow a stapler, I slip out of my chair and scoot around our desk square to Stacey.

"You have to give me a dare," I whisper to her.

Stacey looks up from sharpening her pencil. "Didn't you get a card?" Stacey asks.

"Yes," I say. "But it was . . . hard to read. So you have to give me a new dare or else I'll get double-dog dared for not doing the first one. Quick! Before Mr. Crow gets back."

Stacey nods. Then she starts thinking. Suddenly her eyes brighten and she says, "I've got it! I dare you to empty my pencil sharpener into Mr. Crow's teacup!" Stacey holds her little pencil sharpener out to me. It's made out of clear plastic, so I can see lots of curly shavings inside.

"But what if he drinks them?"

Stacey shrugs. "I'm sure a few pencil shavings won't kill him. Besides, he will probably spit them out right away, which will make everyone laugh!"

"Except Mr. Crow," I mumble.

Stacey makes the sharpener dance in front of my eyes. "Do it!" she says. "I *dare* you!"

I grab the pencil sharpener and hurry to Mr. Crow's desk before I can change my mind. I sprinkle the shavings into his tea and drop the sharpener into Stacey's hand as I race back to my desk.

Chapter
9

When it's time for our second recess, we all meet at the snow fort to report on our dares.

"I hid Mr. Crow's stapler," Meeka says. "If you need to staple anything, look behind the hamster cage."

"I put pencil shavings in his tea," I say. "I mean, in Mr. Crow's tea, not the hamster's." I glance at Stacey. She gives me the thumbs-up.

"I put a snowball in Rusty's backpack," Randi says, laughing. "Who came up with that one?"

Meeka raises her hand.

"Genius," Randi says.

"I had to ask Zane if I could borrow his eraser," Jolene says. She does a little shiver. "It was seriously slimy."

We all laugh.

"Who wrote 'This is stupid' for a dare?" Brooke asks.

"Me," Jenna says.

Brooke squints. "Well, thanks a lot," she says. "Because of you I had to dare myself to give Quinn my school picture."

"What's so bad about that?" Randi asks.

"He drew a mustache and bushy eyebrows on it and then showed it to all the boys." Brooke flicks back her hair.

"So that's what all the commotion was about," Meeka says.

"Uh-huh," Brooke says. "I was totally mummified."

"Mortified?" I say.

"Yes," Brooke says. "That." She turns to Jenna again. "So, did you do one? Or do we get to double-dog dare you?"

Jenna doesn't answer.

"Um . . ." I say. "I think I saw Jenna doing one of mine." I look at Jenna. "You . . . um . . . switched books around in the reading corner, right?"

Jenna glances at me. She nods. Then she glances away.

"Hmph," Brooke says. "That's not much of a dare."

"It was the best I could come up with on short notice," I say.

"What's next?" Jolene asks.

"It's time to pick new dares," Brooke says. She pulls off a mitten and digs the rest of the dare cards out of her coat pocket. She deals them out. "Keep them a secret until tomorrow."

We read the cards to ourselves as we walk back to class. Brooke does a little gasp when she reads hers. I wonder what she will have to do tomorrow. I wonder what *I* will have to do.

I flip over my dare card and do a little gasp too.

I stop and read it again.

At lunch, stand up and yell, "There's a mouse in my macaroni!"

"It's a beauty, ain't it?" Randi says, looking over my shoulder at the card. "Ten times better than the other two I wrote." She gives my back a friendly pat and runs ahead.

I catch up to Stacey and pull her away from the others.

"What did you get?" I whisper to her.

"Stick chalk in Mr. Crow's eraser," Stacey whispers back. "Easy cheesy. How about you?"

"Well, it's definitely cheesy," I say. I glance up to make sure the other girls aren't hanging around. Then I give my dare card to Stacey.

Her eyes go wide as she reads it. Then her mouth cracks into a big smile. "That is sooooo funny!" she says.

"*Funny?*" I say back. "You know how Mrs. Kettleson feels about kids yelling in the lunchroom. She will probably come after me with a spatula."

"But if she doesn't catch you, everyone will think you were very brave for doing it. Even the boys. Won't that be great?"

"The greatest," I mumble. If only being brave didn't mean getting in trouble, and fitting in didn't mean sticking out.

As soon as I get off the bus I want to run right home and think of a way to convince my parents that we should move away. Today, if possible.

But I can't run because I'm walking Rachel to my house.

"C'mon, Rachel," I call over my shoulder. It's the third time I've called to her since we got off the bus. Since Jenna decided to walk with us to the corner.

"When my mom asked *me* to walk Rachel to and from piano lessons, I said *no way,*" Jenna tells me.

"I guess that's why she asked me to do it," I reply.

"And you said *yes*? Just like that?" Jenna asks.

"Just like that," I reply.

Jenna's nose flares. "Well, I just said *no*. It's not like I have time to walk all the way to your house, and then wait around until Rachel's done, and then walk her all the way home again."

I stop at the corner and turn to Jenna. "Why do you always do that?"

"Do what?" Jenna asks.

"Say *no* all the time. Don't you ever wonder what it would be like to say *yes* for a change?"

I do the nose flare too, and wait for Jenna to answer.

But she doesn't. She just walks in a wide circle

around me and heads down the sidewalk to her house.

I glance back at Rachel, but she still isn't coming. She's kneeling on the curb studying a stream of melting snow that's trickling through a metal grate.

"You don't want to be late for your first piano lesson," I call back to her. "My mom will give you a treat if you're on time." I don't mention that my mom gives treats to all of her students just for showing up.

Rachel looks up from the snow stream. "Where does all that water go?" she asks.

I sigh and take a few steps toward her. "You know," I say. "Into a pipe. Then to a river. Then to the nearest ocean."

"The *ocean*?" Rachel says, squinting through the grate. "Down *there*?"

"Yep," I say. "Now come on, or I'm leaving without you." I take a fake step away.

Rachel stands up. She unwinds her scarf and dips the fringe through the grate. "Here, sharkie, sharkie," she says.

I sigh and trudge toward her again. "Rachel,

you can't catch a shark with a scarf. Not unless it tastes like tuna."

Rachel pulls the scarf out and gives the fringe a sniff. She looks at me. "Do you got any tuna?"

"Yes," I say. "At my *house*. Where we were supposed to be five minutes ago." I make my face go all responsible.

Rachel loops her scarf over her head and winds it around her neck. Then she picks up a stick that's poking through the slushy snow and drops it through the grate. "Bye, stick," she says. "Watch out for whales."

She heads down the sidewalk toward my house. "C'mon, Ida!" she calls. "Or I'll be late!"

My mom opens the front door when we finally get to my house. "I was beginning to wonder if you two were lost."

"No," I say. "We were just doing a little . . . fishing."

"Fishing?" Mom says.

Rachel nods. "For sharks!"

Mom helps Rachel with her coat. "Did you catch any?"

"Nope," Rachel says. "We didn't have any tuna. Do you got some?"

Mom smiles. "I'm fresh out," she says. "But I do have cookies. I wonder if sharks like cookies?"

"I bet they do," Rachel says. "I bet they would even like two."

Mom does a little laugh. "Two cookies," she says. "After your lesson."

Rachel smiles and kicks off her boots. She follows Mom into the living room, where we keep our piano.

I dump my stuff and head for the cookies. I take three. One for me, one for George, and one for my fish.

"Cookie, George?" I ask as I plop down next to him on my bed.

George passes, so I take care of it for him.

I walk over to my fish tank and pick up the little container of fish food. I hold a cookie and the fish food up to the tank. "Choose," I say.

My fish swims up to the fish food and taps the glass.

"Good boy," I say. I pop the cookie into my mouth and sprinkle fish food over the water.

I grab my journal, unclip the purple pen, and flip to a blank page. Then I sit on my bed and write TOP SECRET on the page and draw a few lightning bolts. Then I write IF YOU ARE NOT NAMED IDA MAY DO NOT READ PAST THIS POINT! Then I draw a needle with a very sharp point.

Dear Stella,

 We did our dare cards at school today. Only I got a dareless one from Jenna, so Stacey gave me a real one. I guess Mr. Crow drank the pencil shavings I put in his tea, because I never saw him spit all day. Maybe he thought they were tea leaves. I hope he doesn't get pencil poisoning. I hope he doesn't find out I put them there.

 Tomorrow I have to yell that there's a mouse in my macaroni during lunch. Stacey thinks it will be sooooo funny. I wish she wouldn't think it's such a little thing, when it's a big thing to me.

Bye,
Ida

"I'm back," I say after walking Rachel home.

"Good," Mom replies. She's sitting by our piano, writing notes on a sheet of paper. "Thanks."

"You're welcome," I say. "I'm happy to do it, even though you're not paying me."

Mom glances up and smiles. "I appreciate that." Then she pauses and narrows her eyes. She does this when she's studying something. Right now, the thing she is studying is me. Mostly my face. Mostly just my eyes.

"What?" I ask. "Is it marker again?" I lick my fingers and rub my forehead.

"No," Mom says, still studying me. "I was just wondering . . . have you been, by any chance, wearing makeup at school?"

I blink. Several times. "Um . . . what?"

Mom sets down her pencil. "Rachel said she saw you in the hallway a few days ago and your eyelids looked like tropical fish."

I scratch my neck. "Oh," I say. "*That* makeup." I do a little yawn. "Brooke brought some eye shadow to school and everyone borrowed it. No big deal."

"Brooke is allowed to wear makeup?" Mom asks.

I scratch some more. "Only for recitals and stuff," I mumble. "You're not going to tell her mom are you?"

"No," Mom says. "But I think you're too young to be wearing makeup at school. And it's not a good idea to share it, especially not eye makeup."

Mom starts explaining about eye germs, but all I hear is *you're too young* over and over again.

"Mom," I say when she's done with her germ speech. "Some of the girls in my class get to wear fake ponytails, okay? Some of them have had their ears pierced since they were *three*. So I think it's pretty unfair for you to say I'm too young for stuff when I'm the same age as them."

I cross my arms and take a breath.

"I'm not saying you're too young for *everything*," Mom replies, all calm. "Just for some things."

"Well, I should get to decide what I'm *not* too young for," I say.

Mom sits back in her chair and crosses her arms too. "For example?"

I do the breath again because I hadn't planned

on her asking me for examples. If I say something too big I won't get very far.

"I should get to choose my own clothes without you giving me that *look*," I say.

"What look?" Mom asks.

I scrunch up my eyes like someone just turned on a very bright light. *"That orange top clashes with your red skirt, Ida,"* I say in my mom voice. *"And toe socks aren't meant to be worn with flip-flops."*

Mom laughs. "Fair enough," she says. "Starting tomorrow you may choose your own outfits and I will do my best to keep my eye comments to myself."

I suck in one cheek. I know I should quit while I'm ahead, but instead I hear myself say, "And I should get to wear makeup if I want to. *And* get my ears pierced."

Mom's laugh fades away. The only sound I hear is the scritch-scratch of my fingernails against my neck.

"Nail polish, yes," Mom says. "Makeup, no. Bracelets now and earrings when you're ten."

"But everyone—" I start to say.

Mom holds up her hand like a crossing guard.

"I don't want you to make choices based on what everyone else is doing. There's nothing wrong with saving some things for when you're older. Besides, getting your ears pierced means you have to take care of them so they don't get infected. And that means being *responsible*."

I do a big snort. "I am *very* responsible," I say. "I just walked Rachel all the way home without losing her once!"

Mom drums her fingers against her arm. "Yes, but your room is a mess. You still haven't written thank-you notes to Aunt Margo and Grandma May for the Christmas gifts they gave you." She pauses, and narrows her eyes. "And what about your *fish*?"

I narrow my eyes back. "What about him?"

"I keep asking you to clean the tank filter, but you haven't done it yet, have you?"

"I've *thought* about doing it lots of times," I say.

"Thinking and doing aren't the same thing, Ida. And what about a name for the fish? Or are you still *thinking* about that too?"

"Mom," I say, "you don't rush into naming a

fish, or you get stuck with something like *Goldie* or *Flipper*."

Mom sighs. She picks up a stack of music and fusses with it until all the edges are straight. "If you can't do what's needed to take care of a pet, Ida, I don't think you're ready for other big-girl things."

My heart is pounding so hard it makes my ears ring. Actually, it's the doorbell that's ringing, but still, I'm pretty mad.

Mom gets up from her chair and rests her hands on my shoulders. "Here's the deal," she says. "You clean the fish filter and I'll take you and your Christmas money shopping for a new outfit on Saturday. Tops, bottoms, bangles--the works— and I won't give you *the look* once." She does the look as an example. "But makeup and pierced ears will have to *wait*."

I think about how much I would like to choose a whole outfit all by myself. Maybe I could even talk her into letting me get jingle bell boots and a fake ponytail. But instead I make myself say, "I will probably be too busy to go shopping with you."

"Oh?" she says, sliding her hands off my shoulders and walking to the front door, which is still ringing.

I make my face go very smooth. "I have sledding plans."

Mom glances back at me and then opens the door. A piano kid comes in. He kicks off his boots and dumps his coat. Mom points toward the piano and he trudges past me in soggy socks, plopping down on the bench.

"Suit yourself," Mom says, brushing past me. "But *I* plan to go shopping at the mall on Saturday morning."

I do not storm out of the room.

I just turn around and do a slow stomp up the stairs.

I give my bedroom door a very small slam.

Chapter
10

Dear Stella,

I didn't sleep so good last night partly because I have been feeling a little bad about arguing with my mom, and partly because I checked the school's lunch menu that we keep on the fridge. I was hoping for Salisbury steak today, even though I hate it. Because guess what we are having?

Macaroni and cheese.

When I start yelling about a mouse in my macaroni it will really sound true. Which will make everyone else start yelling, too. And when Mrs. Kettleson comes out of the kitchen to see what all the yelling is about and doesn't find one tiny paw or pink tail in my macaroni . . . I'm in for it. Mrs. Kettleson is not a big fan of

yelling unless she's the one doing it.
Bye (maybe forever),
Ida

I see Stacey before school, but I don't mention my dare because all the other girls are around. Plus, I'm still thinking about what happened earlier at the bus stop.

We were all just standing there, not talking because it was cold and sometimes it feels warmer if you bury your chin in your collar and don't move your lips. But then Tess did a big sneeze. A monster sneeze. Her face was snot city. So was her coat.

She looked at Quinn for help, but he just shook his head and said, "Nu-uh. No way." So I started fishing around in my pocket for a tissue even though I'm not a big fan of cleaning up snot, but before I could even check both pockets, Jenna said, "Here," and handed Tess a handkerchief made out of actual cloth. Tess took it and tried to wipe her face, but it didn't work very well because it's hard to grip a hankie with mittens on.

So Jenna picked the hankie up off the ground and wiped Tess's face and cleaned the splatters off her coat, even though they were already frozen on, but still, she tried. Then Jenna bunched up the hankie and stuffed it back in her pocket.

I was mostly in shock. Partly because she kept all that snot, and partly because she had helped Tess without anyone telling her to.

I'm still wondering what has gotten into her when I sit down at my desk. But then Randi walks by making squeaky mouse sounds, so my mind gets right back to worrying about lunch again.

I'm dreading lunch so much, I can hardly even enjoy the other girls doing their dares. I barely giggle when Mr. Crow erases the board and leaves chalk streaks behind. When Jolene "accidentally" lets our hamster loose and it takes most of math to catch him, I don't smile at all even though missing math is one of my favorite things to do.

But, worse yet, when Brooke touches Dylan's shoe and then howls all the way to our classroom sink, I'm so busy keeping my worry locked inside,

I can't even open my mouth to laugh along with everyone else.

"What is going *on*?" Mr. Crow asks sharply. He hands Brooke a wet wipe and sends her back to her desk. "First there's chalk in my eraser. Then the hamster gets out. Yesterday, I found pencil shavings in my tea, and now Brooke is acting like she touched hazardous waste."

Mr. Crow steps to the front of the classroom. He crosses his arms and gives us all a very serious squint. "Anyone care to enlighten me?"

All the boys shrug.

All the girls count ceiling tiles.

When it's time for lunch, I stand in line between Quinn and Tom, wondering what I should do. If I ask Stacey to help me get out of the dare, she will probably tell me to stop worrying because everyone will think it's so funny. Randi will think it's funny, I know, because she's the one who thought up the dare. And Brooke will think it's funny because Stacey does. And probably Meeka and Jolene will agree.

The only one left to wonder about is Jenna. I

112

glance at her. She's standing in line ahead of Tom, holding her lunchbox. Will she think it's funny if I yell in the lunchroom?

Part of me answers *yes* and part of me answers *no*.

I decide to let the *no* part of me be the boss for a little while, and ask Tom if I can cut in line. He says okay, so I scoot around him and tap Jenna on the shoulder.

Jenna glances back at me. "What?"

"Um . . . I was wondering if maybe I could trade my hot lunch for your cold lunch today." Jenna's cold lunches almost always include bread that looks like it was made from twigs, soy milk, and tofu brownies. But I'm pretty desperate.

Jenna turns. "*You* want to eat *my* lunch?"

"Uh-huh," I say. "Just this once."

"But you love macaroni and cheese," she replies.

"Yes, but I've heard that too much dairy can make you moody." I do my best moody face.

Jenna squints. "This doesn't have anything to do with your *dare,* does it?"

I gulp. "No."

"Because Randi told everyone to keep an eye on you at lunch."

I gulp again. "Well, maybe it has a *tiny* bit to do with my dare. But if you trade lunches with me, it would help a lot."

"But if I help you get out of doing a dare, then we'll *both* get double-dog dared."

"I know," I mumble. Then I sigh. I think about this morning and how Jenna helped Tess with her snot problem. It's hard enough for me to get a mean person into trouble. It's even harder when it's someone who was recently nice. "Never mind," I say.

Jenna lifts her chin. "I didn't say I wouldn't help you. I only said it might get us into trouble with the other girls."

"So, does that mean you *will* help me?"

Jenna shifts her jaw back and forth, thinking. "What about Stacey?" she asks. "She's your best friend. Shouldn't *she* help you?"

"I asked her to," I say. "I mean, I meant to. But some other stuff got in the way." I glance behind me and see Stacey talking with Brooke. "I guess I could ask her now, but—"

"Fine," Jenna cuts in. "Ask her." She turns away quickly and one of her braids whips against my cheek. It leaves behind a sting.

I rub my cheek and watch Jenna push past people to get into the lunchroom.

The line moves forward. I head back to Stacey.

But before I can get to her, someone squeezes my arm.

"Lunch is *this* way," Randi says, tugging on me. "You don't want to miss *mouseroni* and cheese, do you?" She gives me a grin.

"No," I say. "Of course not. I was just—"

Randi turns me around and steers me toward the trays.

Each tray has five food compartments—three squares, one circle, and one big rectangle.

The squares get peas and carrots, a pudding cup, and a carton of chocolate milk. The circle gets a buttered bun.

The rectangle gets enough macaroni and cheese to feed twenty mice.

I walk over to our usual table. Jenna is already there. So are Meeka and Jolene. I sit down, leaving a chair between me and Jenna. Randi sits across from me. A minute later, Stacey and Brooke show up. Brooke slides in next to Randi. Stacey takes the empty chair between me and Jenna. "Yum," Stacey says. "Lunch looks good today."

"Oh, it's good," Randi says, scooping up a forkful of cheesy noodles. "Go ahead, Ida. Dig in." She stuffs the saucy noodles into her mouth and watches me while she chews.

I blink at my tray. Each noodle curves like Randi's grin. I scoop a few into my mouth and swallow them like medicine.

The other girls start talking about Mr. Crow and how mad he was this morning.

"I'll never tell him what's going on," Brooke says. "Even if it means getting detention for a week."

"A month," Jolene adds.

"A *year*," Meeka chimes in.

Randi nudges me under the table and nods toward my macaroni. "Go on," she whispers. "Do it."

I take a sip of milk.

And feel another nudge.

This time it's from Stacey. "What's wrong?" she asks, studying my face. "You look sort of . . . queasy. Does the milk taste like cardboard again?"

"Uh-huh," I say, and set down my carton.

Stacey scoops up a forkful of peas and carrots. "You should take it back and complain," she says. "That's what I'd do."

"Uh-huh," I say again.

I push back my chair.

Stacey munches and gives me the thumbs-up. Randi gives me the thumbs-up too.

I stand and shut my eyes.

I suck in every inch of air my lungs can hold.

Then I shout, "THERE'S A MOUSE IN MY MACARONI!"

Only my throat muscles are pinched so tight, the words come out small and squeaky.

But even a small squeak spreads in a lunch-room.

Especially when Randi Peterson has told everyone to keep an eye on me.

Chairs slide. Trays clatter. I open my eyes and see a crowd of kids gathering around me.

"Look!" someone shouts. "There *is* a mouse!"

I look down at my tray. A white mouse slowly sinks into my noodles. Its rubber tail is tipped with saucy cheese.

"Mouse! Mouse in the macaroni!" someone shouts. Everyone joins in. Fists pounding. Trays clanking.

I look at Randi.

She looks back and wiggles her eyebrows.

Suddenly, all the pounding and clanking and shouting stops. The kids who are crowded closest to me back away to let someone through.

Someone with pea-sized eyes behind thick glasses. Meaty arms. And a black hairnet clamped over her gray hair.

"QUIET!" Mrs. Kettleson shouts. "No yelling in the lunchroom!"

She pushes to my side and sees the mouse on my tray. "What's *this*?!" she blasts. A moment later the mouse is dangling in front of my face.

Everyone explodes with laughter.

Not counting me.

Not counting Mrs. Kettleson.

She grabs my arm and starts pulling me through the crowd.

"Wait!" I hear someone shout. *"Waaaait!"*

Mrs. Kettleson stops and we both turn toward the shout.

"Ida didn't do it!"

It's Stacey. My best friend. Sticking up for me.

Mrs. Kettleson squeezes my arm tighter. "Then who did?"

"Um . . ." Stacey says, glancing around. Her eyes hopscotch from kid to kid until they finally land on Randi.

Stacey turns to Mrs. Kettleson. "It was . . . one of the boys."

This isn't the first time Stacey has lied. But it's the first time she's lied to get me out of trouble.

Mrs. Kettleson pushes her glasses up on her nose and scans the crowd. "Which boy?" she asks.

"Um . . ." Stacey says. "It was . . . it was . . ."

"*That* one," someone says.

I look past Stacey to see where the voice is coming from. Everyone else looks too.

A chair squeaks against the floor and Jenna Drews stands up. But she doesn't stop there. She climbs right up onto her chair. She punches her fists into her hips and waits until everyone is looking at her. Then she points a finger at one face in the crowd.

A boy face.

A Quinn face.

"He did it," Jenna says. "Quinn put the mouse in Ida's macaroni."

Quinn's face sags. "Huh?" he says. "I did not!"

Mrs. Kettleson huffs. "We'll see about that." She stuffs the mouse into her apron pocket and reaches for Quinn.

Then she hauls both of us to the principal's office.

Chapter
11

I'm sitting on one of the hard metal chairs in the main office. Mrs. Kettleson has already gone into Ms. Stevens's office to tell her why I'm here. The door is closed tight, but some of Mrs. Kettleson's words leak out. Words like *shouting*, *trouble*, and *fed up.*

My face feels red hot, but my hands are ice cold. It's hard to swallow because my heart is pounding in my throat. Not that I have any spit to swallow. My mouth is drier than Mrs. Kettleson's corn bread. What am I going to tell Ms. Stevens?

I watch the clock that hangs above Ms. Rivera's head. She's sitting at her secretary's desk, typing on her computer like this is just another ordinary day. The big hand on the clock moves ahead a notch. It feels like each notch equals one hour instead of one minute. I'm glad about this and not glad at the same time.

"You okay?" I hear someone say.

I look at Ms. Rivera. She tips her chin and studies me over the top of her blue-rimmed glasses.

I nod. "It's just that I've never been sent to the principal's office before. Not ever. It's something I work really hard at not doing even though Ms. Stevens doesn't seem so bad. Still, if it was up to me, I'd rather do anything else than talk to her right now. Even fractions. Even dodge ball." I'm babbling like crazy, but I can't help it.

Ms. Rivera gives me a sympathetic smile. Then she goes back to typing.

I glance at Quinn. He's sitting next to me on another hard chair, bouncing his feet against the chair legs like tether balls. "Is this your first time too?" I ask him.

Quinn bumps the back of his head against the wall in time to his swinging feet. "Second," he says.

"When was the first?"

Quinn stops swinging and bumping. He

glances sideways at me. "Remember last year? When all the kickballs got stuck on the roof?"

I nod. "The playground monitor made us all stand by the school wall and think about how boring recess is without kickballs." I pause. "You kicked them up there?"

Quinn nods. "Me and Rusty."

"Why?" I ask.

Quinn shrugs. "Why not?"

The door to Ms. Stevens's office opens and she steps out. "Ida?"

She says my name like it's a question, but I don't answer. I just slide off my chair. It feels like my heart slides right out of my chest and onto the floor.

Mrs. Kettleson steps out and gives me a smile. It's not the sympathetic kind. "I'm telling you, Ms. Stevens," she says, "it's the quiet ones you've got to watch out for."

"I'm sure we'll get things straightened out, won't we, Ida?" Ms. Stevens says.

I nod, partly because I really do want everything to be straight again and partly because my neck is the only bone I can move.

Mrs. Kettleson looks at Quinn and frowns. "And that one," she says. "He needs watching too."

"I didn't do anything," Quinn grumbles.

"We'll see about that," Mrs. Kettleson says again, and huffs out the door.

Ms. Stevens motions to me. "You first, Ida," she says.

I take a step toward Ms. Stevens, but then I stop and glance back at Quinn. "I know you didn't do it," I whisper to him.

Quinn starts swinging his feet again.

I walk inside Ms. Stevens's office.

"Have a seat," she says, closing the door.

I sink into a chair by her desk. It's a lot softer than the waiting chair. At least my butt feels cozy.

Ms. Stevens sits behind her tidy desk. The only things on it are a couple stacks of paper, a Purdee Panthers mug filled with pens and pencils, a telephone, and a rubber mouse.

Ms. Stevens looks tidy too. Her hair fits her head like a brown knit cap. It angles toward her square chin. She laces her long fingers on top of her desk. Her fingernails aren't chewed up at all. They're painted pink.

I pick at the last bit of gold polish on the tips of my stubby fingernails. It's all that's left from the last time Stacey spent the night at my house. The night we were both angels in the Purdee Holiday Pageant. We painted our nails gold to match our tinsel halos and wings.

"Why don't you tell me about what happened in the lunchroom," Ms. Stevens says.

I look away and see a picture on her wall of trees and a river and hills. The colors all blend together and I wonder if maybe the artist used oil pastels to draw it. I wonder if it's a drawing of a real place and if I could fly there right now.

"Ida?" Ms. Stevens says my name like a question again.

"I guess I yelled," I say. "A little."

Ms. Stevens leans forward in her chair. The only thing between me and her is the rubber mouse. "What did you yell?"

I sink deeper in my chair. "'There's a mouse in my macaroni'?"

"And *was* there a mouse in your macaroni?" Ms. Stevens asks.

I shake my head. "Not a real one."

Ms. Stevens picks up the rubber mouse. It has dried cheese sauce on its tail. "Ida, why would you put a toy mouse in your macaroni?"

"I didn't," I say.

"Then who did? Quinn?"

I bite my bottom lip. And shake my head slowly. "Quinn didn't do anything wrong," I say. "Not since the kickball incident."

Ms. Stevens leans back in her chair. "Ida," she says. "It's important that you tell me the whole story so we can set things straight." She runs her finger along the edge of her desk, drawing an invisible line from one point to another and back again. Her mouth is a straight line too. It's not a frown line, but it's not a smile line either. "Who put the mouse in your macaroni?" she asks again.

I try to think up a story to tell her. One that's partly true and partly not. Like Stacey sometimes tells. The kind of story that will keep me out of trouble with the other girls.

But I'm not as good at making up stories as Staccy is.

"Ida," Ms. Stevens says again. "I'm afraid that if you don't tell me the truth, I'll have to call your parents and give you detention. I know Mrs. Kettleson won't settle for anything less. And, frankly, I won't either."

Ms. Stevens keeps talking, but I'm not really listening. What will my mom say when she gets that phone call from Ms. Stevens? What will she think? And my dad . . . This is just one more example of how not responsible I am.

Having my parents mad at me feels almost as bad as having my friends mad at me.

Maybe even worse.

Ms. Stevens puts her hand on the telephone. "I'll give you one more chance, Ida. Who put the mouse in your macaroni?"

I shut my eyes to keep the tears inside.

"It was Randi," I say so softly, it's like I only breathed it. "But she only did it because of the game."

"What game?"

"Truth or dare," I say. "We're all playing it."

"All?"

I open my eyes and nod. "All the girls."

Ms. Stevens taps her fingers on the phone like she finally found what she was looking for.

She picks it up. And punches three numbers.

"Mr. Crow?" she says. "It's Ms. Stevens. I have a little . . . situation I need to clear up. Would you please send all the girls from your class down to my office? Ida is already here."

Ms. Stevens sets down the phone and says, "Thank you, Ida."

"You're welcome," I reply, even though *I'm* not feeling very welcome at all.

In fact, I feel like the most unwelcome girl in the world because I know what I've done.

I've spilled the beans.

"I'm sorry," I say to Stacey for the millionth time as we walk to my bus after school. "I didn't mean to tell on everyone. It just spilled out."

"It's okay," she says back, for the million and oneth time. "I'm not mad at you. No one is."

I sigh. Each time she says it, the words feel like they get wrapped tighter and tighter around my words. Like a rubber band you wrap around your finger until the tip turns purple.

"But we had to apologize to Mrs. Kettleson," I say. "And to Mr. Crow. And we can't play truth or dare at school anymore. And it's all my fault."

"It's no big deal," Stacey says, stopping by my bus.

Kids bump past us and climb on. I glance up and see Jenna watching us through a circle in the frost on her window. She glances away.

"I should have just told Ms. Stevens that *I* put the mouse on my tray and started yelling about it all by myself. Then nobody else would have gotten into trouble."

"You're not a yeller, Ida," Stacey says. "She would have figured it out."

I sigh and glance up at the bus again.

Jenna glances away again.

I turn to Stacey. "Call me later?"

"Um . . ." Stacey says, "I better not."

"Why?"

"Well, *I'm* not mad at you, of course, but some of the other girls might be a little . . . upset. And if they found out I called you, it might make them . . . upsetter."

"Who's upset?" I ask. "Brooke? And how would she find out you called me, unless you told her?"

Stacey is quiet for a moment. She sticks her hands deep into the pockets of her silver jacket and does a little shiver. "Brrrrr," she says. "I better go before we turn into Popsicles. I'll *try* to call you tonight. I promise."

I nod and give her a wave. "Bye," I say.

"Bye," Stacey says back. Then she turns around and jingles away.

I climb on the bus. The driver shuts the door.

I'm the last one on, so it's crowded. I slide in next to Jenna.

The bus pulls away from the curb and we rumble down the street.

"Thanks for trying to get me out of trouble at lunch," I say, glancing at Jenna.

"I didn't try to get you out of trouble," Jenna says. "I was trying to get Quinn *into* trouble. For calling me a baby last week."

"Oh," I say. "Sorry. My mistake."

I pick at a crack in the seat cushion. "But if

130

you wanted to get back at someone," I say, "why not Randi? She's the one who put the mouse on my tray, plus she made you tell Zane that you like him."

"That was on Monday," Jenna says. "Quinn teased me about sucking my thumb last week. You have to get back at people in the right order."

The bus turns a corner and then slows to a stop. A couple of little kids get off and we start moving again.

Jenna glances at me. "Stacey's mad at you, isn't she?"

"No," I say. "She's not mad."

Jenna clicks her tongue and looks away. She puts the side of her bare fist on the bus window, holding it against the frost.

I give her left braid a frown. "Why?" I say. "Do you think she's mad?"

Jenna shrugs and pulls her fist away, leaving a curved shape in the frost. She melts five fingertip circles at the top of the shape. Altogether, it looks like a little footprint. "It's just . . . you know," she says. "She didn't squeeze your arm."

I do a snort. "So?"

Jenna turns to me. "So-o," she says, "Stacey *always* squeezes the other person's arm when she says good-bye. Haven't you noticed?"

I fidget a little. "No."

"Well, she does." Jenna looks past me and does a big sparkly smile. A Stacey smile. "Bye! . . . *squeeze*. Bye! . . . *squeeze*. Bye! . . . *squeeze*." She squeezes her hand into a fist each time she says it. Then she makes her face go normal again. "It's like a *pattern* with her."

Jenna turns back to the window and presses her fist against the glass.

I face forward and rub my unsqueezed arm.

"She's not mad at me," I say.

Jenna clicks her tongue again.

Dear Stella,

    Today was the worst day of my life. Even worse than that time I got my toe caught in those bike spokes. Today I got sent to the principal's office! The only good thing about getting sent there was that Ms. Stevens didn't tell my parents. I don't plan on telling them either.

But the bad thing was I spilled the beans on my friends. We all got in trouble for playing truth or dare, and now everyone is secretly mad at me. Even Stacey. At least that's what Jenna thinks, and I'm starting to think so too. Partly because Stacey did not squeeze my arm good-bye, and partly because all of the other girls said "We're not mad!" all sweet and swirly. Like cotton candy. But when they turned away it was like their words melted into nothing.

The only one who doesn't seem mad is Jenna. In fact, she seems happy that everyone else is mad.

I guess that's typical for a frenemy.

Bye,
Ida

P.S. Stacey promised she would try to call me tonight. But she didn't.

Chapter

12

When class starts the next day I try to pretend like everything is normal even though I know it isn't. I keep catching the other girls' glances. Sometimes they smile, but they aren't the kind that stick. No one is mean to me, but no one is going out of their way to be nice to me either.

And guess who gets to be the odd girl out when Mr. Crow tells us to pair up and do an English worksheet? Me. No one invites me to triple up. Not even Stacey, who is with Brooke.

During recess, I memorize all the messages written on the inside of the third stall in the girls' bathroom.

GS + V R
CU L8R!
KAI = X BF

It takes me until the bell rings to do the whole stall, which means I don't have time to meet up with the other girls at the snow fort.

At lunch it feels like everyone is reading from a script instead of just talking. Like they're afraid that a microphone is hidden in the pocket of my hoodie and everything they say is being pumped straight to Ms. Stevens's office.

When it's time for our second recess, I memorize the second bathroom stall.

After school, I walk with Stacey through the park to Miss Woo's dance studio. Stacey has dance class today with all the other girls, except Randi. And me. The other girls aren't walking with us, like they usually do.

We stop in front of the Purdee Good Café. It's right across the street from Miss Woo's. We always meet here after Stacey's done with dance and share a giant cookie. Then, when Stacey's mom is done working, she gives me a ride home.

Thursdays are the best days because of the giant cookies. And all the stuff that goes with them.

But today when we stop in front of the café

something feels different. Like the air between us is colder than usual, and not just because it's winter.

I grab the handle on the door, but I don't pull it open. I glance at Stacey. "See you after dance?" I say.

"Um . . ." Stacey says. "I can't today." She taps snow off her boots. Her jingle bell laces dance and ring.

I squeeze the handle tighter. "Why not?"

"Because . . . um . . . Brooke invited me over to her house so we can start planning our shapes snack. We both got circles."

Mr. Crow assigned all of us geometric shapes today. Circles, triangles, squares. Even stars. Next week, we have to bring a snack to share that looks like our shape.

"But circles are easy," I say. "Practically every snack is shaped like one. Cookies. Donuts. Bananas, if you slice them. Besides, we don't have to bring the snacks until Monday. Can't you and Brooke do it over the weekend?"

Stacey taps her boots again. "Sorry," she says. "I already promised." Stacey glances across the

136

street and waves to Brooke, Meeka, and Jolene. They watch us for a moment, then slip inside Miss Woo's. "Plus, there's something else."

"What?"

"We had a secret meeting in the snow fort today. Brooke decided you can't be in our group anymore. Not unless you do a triple-dog dare."

My eyes start to sting and I blink fast. "What did you say?"

"I said it's no fair for one person to decide that, so . . . we did a vote."

"And? Did you vote me out?"

Stacey nods. "Not *me*, of course. But it was four against two so, you know, majority rules."

I let my hand fall from the handle.

Stacey starts to cross the street. She stops and turns. "I'm sorry, Ida," she says. "Really. I'll still be your friend even if you don't do a triple-dog dare, okay?"

I nod and blink faster. But not fast enough to keep up with my tears.

Stacey is all the way across the street when I suddenly remember something she said about the vote. She said it was four to *two*.

"Stacey!" I yell. "Who else voted to keep me in?"

But Stacey's already headed into Miss Woo's.

I wipe my eyes and step inside the Purdee Good.

Brooke's sister, Jade, and another high school girl, Meghan, are huddled at the counter, talking fast to each other. They look up when I walk in. When they see that it's just me, they go back to talking.

"One skinny mocha, extra cream," Kelli says, setting a mug that's as big as a cereal bowl in front of Jade. "And one chocolate chai with cream, hold the nutmeg." She sets another mug in front of Meghan.

"Thank you!" Jade and Meghan say together. They lift the mugs to their lips and start sucking cream.

There's an empty stool next to Jade, so I put my backpack on it and scoot onto the next one over. I pull off my gloves, but I don't bother to take off my coat and hat. In fact, I wonder why I'm hanging around at all since Stacey isn't going to show up. I think about calling my mom to see if she will come and get me. I could walk home from here, but my legs aren't feeling very walkable right now.

"Rough day?" Kelli asks. She wipes up a ring of water on the counter and gives me a smile.

I nod.

Kelli leans in, resting her elbows on the counter. She smells spicy. Probably from all the cooking that goes on around here. And fruity. Probably from all the gel in her short, spiky hair. It's a friendly way to smell.

"Will a cookie help?" she asks.

"Probably not," I say, pulling off my hat and setting it on my backpack. "But I'll have one anyway."

Kelli walks over to a glass case that sits at the far end of the counter. She takes out a giant chocolate chip cookie, puts it on a plate, and brings it back to me. "This one has extra chips," she whispers, and sets down the plate.

"Thanks," I say. "Did you know Stacey is going to Brooke's after dance?"

Kelli nods. "She texted me. Something about a homework assignment?"

"Something like that," I say.

139

Kelli picks up a coffeepot. "I can still give you a ride home if you want," she says.

"That's okay," I say back. "I can use the exercise."

Kelli carries the coffeepot to a booth where three women are sharing a slice of lemon meringue pie.

"Want to talk about it?" I hear someone say.

I glance up. Jade is studying me with her very blue eyes. Well, today they're very blue. Sometimes they're very green. Sometimes brown, which I think is her real color.

Meghan does a little snort. She gives Jade a nudge.

Jade lets her perfectly smooth face crack into a sweet smile. Too sweet. The bands on her braces match her black outfit. And her black hair. She cups a few loose strands behind her ear. It's a small ear, like a doll's dish, but she can still fit three earrings on it. Her other ear—the one that's hidden under her hair—is even smaller and curled up tight, like a baby's fist. I know because I saw it once. Jade can't even hear out of it. Brooke told us.

"Talk about what?" I say back.

"You know," Jade says, leaning in. "Your bad day?"

Meghan lets another snort slip.

Jade tries to hide her real smile behind the rim of her coffee mug.

I know they're teasing me. I knew it even before the first snort. Jade can be nice when it's just her and you. Like when she's babysitting. Then she lets you stay up late and watch PG-13 movies, and sometimes she will even paint your toenails if you've taken a bath first. That's how I saw her baby-fist ear. She pulled her hair back with a scrunchy so it wouldn't touch the wet polish.

The door jingles and Randi stomps in. Snow falls from her boots and coat. She pulls off her face mask and gives it a shake.

"Leave any outside?" Kelli asks, walking past Randi to get behind the counter.

"Not much," Randi says, dropping her backpack. She pulls my backpack off the stool and sits down, digging snow out of her collar. "What a wiener," she says, flicking snow onto the floor.

"Who's a wiener?" I ask. "Me?"

"Not you," Randi says. "Rusty." She reaches

141

over and breaks off a chunk of my cookie. "Mind?" she asks, popping the chunk into her mouth.

I scoot the plate toward her. "Why? What did Rusty do?"

"You know that big tree in front of Mrs. Eddy's house?" she asks.

I nod.

"He was hiding behind it. When I walked by he ran out, tackled me, and stuffed a snowball down my neck."

"He must have figured out you put one in his backpack, huh?" I say.

"Huh," Randi replies.

"Can I get you anything?" Kelli asks Randi. "Hot chocolate? Cookie? Towel?"

"No thanks, I'm good," Randi says, breaking off another chunk of my cookie. But I don't mind. I'm just happy she's still talking to me.

The door jingles again and a bunch of boys pile in, talking loud and laughing. Joey, the Dylans, and Rusty.

Randi shoots a look at Rusty. "You are dead meat," she says.

Rusty's eyes and mouth go wide. "What'd I do?" he asks, all innocent.

"Yeah, what'd he do?" Joey chimes in.

The Dylans snort back laughs. They scoot down the counter, order four sodas from Kelli, and gallop to a back booth.

Randi's eyes stay on Rusty. She's frowning, but I can see a grin around the edges.

I break the rest of my cookie down the middle and hold half of it out to her. "Thanks," she says, taking it. "I'm starved. Remind me to bring a cold lunch to school on tuna noodle casserole day."

"Me too," I reply.

Randi munches the cookie. "Not like *mouse-roni* and cheese, huh? Gotta love that." She loosens up a grin.

"I could live without it," I mumble. "In fact, I would eat tuna noodle casserole every day until middle school if it meant everyone would stop being mad at me."

Randi chews for a minute. "Well, there's only one way to fix it," she says. "You gotta do a triple-dog dare."

"I know," I mumble. "Stacey told me. But if I do one, will everything be the same again?"

Randi bobs her head. "Same same."

I think about how much I don't want to be the odd girl out. And how doing one more dare will get me back in.

"Okay," I say. "Do it. Triple-dog dare me."

"Can't," Randi says, brushing crumbs from her coat. She scoots off her stool. "You told on the whole group, so the whole group has to decide on the dare."

"Oh," I say, slouching.

Randi gives my back a friendly pat. "Don't worry," she says. "We'll figure it out tomorrow. When we're finished with you, no one will be mad anymore."

"Um . . . thanks," I say.

Randi gives me another pat. Then she tromps to the back of the café, where the boys are dumping sugar packets into their sodas. She gives Rusty's shoulder a fake punch and he does a fake yelp. Then she squishes in next to him.

Jade and Meghan scoot off their stools and walk past me to the coat tree by the door. Meghan grabs her stuff and says good-bye.

Jade takes a minute to button up her brown wool coat. She winds a bright red scarf around her neck and steps toward me. "What was that all about?" she asks.

I give her a shrug.

"Hello?" she says. "*Mouse*roni and cheese? Triple-dog dare? Everybody mad at you?"

"Oh, that," I say. "It's nothing. Just sort of . . . a game."

"A game, huh?" Jade says. She takes a hat out of her coat pocket and pulls it on. "Sounds more like a *mess* to me."

Dear Stella,

I got voted out of the group today. I can't get back in unless I do a triple-dog dare.

Stacey said she would still be my friend even if I'm not in the group. But that would mean I only get half a best friend because part of her would always be with them.

So I told Randi I would do a triple-dog dare.

Ms. Stevens said we can't do dares at school anymore, so it will have to be something they can make me do after school or on the weekend.

I can think of a million dares that could
happen after school or on a weekend. Drink a
bottle of hot sauce. Hold a sign that says "I like
Quinn." Go sledding with underwear on my head.

I set my journal down on my bed and rub my
eyes because it feels like a tiny hammer is pounding behind them.

It taps out a few tears.

I reach for a tissue and blow my nose.

George tips sideways off my pillow and nudges
against my arm.

"Thanks," I say to him. "I know you want to
help, but I have to do this by myself."

I pick up George and rest my chin on his head.
He still smells like the perfume I sprayed on him
when I was in kindergarten. Back when my biggest worry was getting stuck next to Zane for rest
time because of his drool. And my hardest problem was tying my shoes.

I pick up my journal again.

Mr. Crow gave us homework for next week.
We all have to bring shape snacks to school.

Some kids got easy ones like circles and squares.
But I got a hard one. Hexagons. What can
you eat that has six equal sides? Snowflakes
maybe, but it would take a lot of them to make
a snack.

I'm getting to be an expert at hard stuff.

Chapter

13

The next morning I take extra long getting dressed and eating my breakfast and brushing my teeth so I will accidentally miss the bus. I wait on my porch until I see it go by. Then I wait a few more minutes before I ask my mom if she can drive me.

We get to school just as the bell rings, which is what I was hoping for, since I'm not in the mood for being left out before I even get inside our classroom.

All the girls get together in the snow fort during recess to plan my triple-dog dare. I know because I'm watching them from the top of the monkey bars.

"Won't they let you play with them today?" someone asks.

Tom Sanders climbs up next to me.

I glance away from the snow fort. "No, it's not that. Our fort is just a little small, so I volunteered to play by myself."

"Uh-huh," Tom says.

"What about you?" I ask. "It looks like the other boys are playing king of the mountain."

Tom shrugs and bumps his boot against the metal bar we're standing on. "Not really my game," he says.

Snow chunks fall from Tom's boot and land on two kids below us. They look up and frown.

"Oops," Toms says. "Sorry!"

The kids move away. Tom glances at me. "Do you think they're mad?"

"Probably not," I say. "A few snow chunks on your head is no big deal."

"No, I mean do you think the *girls* are mad," Tom says. "Because you told on them to Ms. Stevens."

I bump my boot against the bar. "You know about that?"

Tom shrugs again. "I might have heard a rumor."

"Some of them might be a little mad," I say,

looking at the snow fort. "But it will all be good as soon as I do . . . something."

"What?" Tom asks.

"A dare," I say. "A triple-dogger. They're planning it now."

We're quiet for a minute. I keep watching the girls. Tom tries a couple chin-ups.

"I could spy on them for you," he finally says. "You know, do a little undercover surveillance?" He wiggles his eyebrows.

It makes me smile. "Thanks, but if you got caught they would probably take you prisoner. And then Jenna would make you talk."

Tom does a snort. "She doesn't scare me anymore," he says. "Not much."

We keep talking and practicing chin-ups until the bell rings. Then I hurry to catch up with Stacey in the coatroom.

"What's my dare?" I whisper to her as we hang up our stuff.

"We didn't pick one yet," she whispers back. "Jenna and Brooke got into a fight over what the dare should be. Jenna said we should make you go down Ricochet Ridge backward, but Brooke said that was too easy and that we shouldn't just rush into picking any old dare because planning it is half the fun. So she told us to all think of dares over the weekend and we'll vote on the best one next week."

"I have to wait until next week?" I say.

Stacey nods. "You know Brooke. She likes everything to be just so."

We head into the classroom. "But we could still go to Ricochet Ridge, even without a dare," I say. "After school, or maybe tomorrow? You could come to my house first and—"

"Um . . . I can't," Stacey says.

"Oh," I say. "Okay. We can just meet there if you want."

"No, I mean I can't go sledding. At all. I'm going to Brooke's after school. Actually, I'm spending the night."

"But you were at Brooke's *last* night," I say.

"I know, but my mom has to work tomorrow and my grandma is busy, so staying at Brooke's will be a big help to them. But we can go sledding on Sunday. Maybe Brooke will even want to come with us! Now that she knows you're going to do a triple-dog dare I'm sure she won't mind being seen with you."

Stacey's eyes go bright like this is the best idea ever. She squeezes my arm before zooming to her desk, but I barely feel it.

Dear Stella,

Jenna tried to pick my dare today, but Brooke said it was too easy. And, actually, it was. I've gone down Ricochet Ridge backward lots of times. Sometimes even on purpose. It's scary, but it's not triple-dog scary. Maybe going down standing up, like Zane did, would be. But backward? I know that's easy cheesy.

And Jenna knows it too.

Stacey went to Brooke's after school. She's even spending the night. She said it's because her mom has to work this weekend.

But I know that's not the whole story.

Stacey wants to go. That's the part she's not telling me.

Bye,
Ida

On Saturday morning I pull the fish filter out a tiny bit to peek at it.

Gunk city. I slide it back in. "Checking it is almost the same as cleaning it, right?" I say to George.

George frowns.

I turn him around and sprinkle fish food in the tank. My fish swims up to nibble the flakes while I duck down to look through the glass. If I look at just the right angle, my fish looks huge.

I think about giving him a big name, like Godzilla or Goliath.

Tom Sanders told me yesterday that goldfish grow depending on how big their tanks are. The bigger the tank, the bigger the fish.

I think about how big my fish would grow if I kept him in the bathtub. Then I could name him Goliath for sure. But my mom and dad probably wouldn't be in favor of that plan.

"I need a smaller name for you," I say, looking at my fish. "Because I think you're stuck being small."

I think about small names, like mine. *Ida.* Only three letters.

My room is pretty small too. One rectangle

bed. One square desk and dresser. One half-moon nightstand. One skinny monkey.

"Maybe people aren't like fish," I say. "Maybe they can grow big even in a small space."

"Ida!" Mom calls from downstairs. "You ready?"

"Almost!" I call back.

When I woke up this morning the first thing I thought about was my triple-dog dare. And what I could do so the girls wouldn't make it too smelly.

Or scary.

Or embarrassing.

And that's when I thought of a way to soften up Brooke. And the others too.

I grab my Christmas money and tuck it inside my bag.

A few minutes later, me and my mom are on our way to the mall.

"New outfit, then?" Mom asks as we drive along.

"Maybe," I say. "But first I want to buy some presents for my friends."

"But you already exchanged presents at school," Mom says.

"Yes, but I want to get them *bonus* presents," I say, "because they are being so nice to me lately."

I reach over and turn up the volume on the radio. Sometimes you don't feel like sharing all the details. Not even with your mother.

When we get inside the mall Mom asks, "Where to?"

"Let's start with the Mish Mosh," I say.

Almost everyone likes the Mish Mosh because the clothes there are very stretchy and sparkly. Sparkly clothes are not always *my* favorite because of how they can also be itchy, but I know I will be able to find presents there that most of the girls will love.

We walk inside the Mish Mosh and music is playing even louder than it was in our car. There's a jewelry bin near the door with a sign hanging above it that says *Sale!* "I want to start there," I tell Mom.

"Okay," she says. "I'll check out the clearance racks."

Mom heads to the back.

I head to the bin.

I start digging through all the earrings, necklaces, bracelets, and rings that are jumbled together.

"Can I help you find anything?" I hear someone say.

I look up and see a saleslady standing by me. Actually, she's more of a salesgirl. Just a little older than Jade. She's chewing gum, which makes her dangly earrings jiggle and shimmer under the bright fluorescent lights.

"No, thank you," I say. "I'm just looking."

"Well, you let me know if you need any help, honey." She walks over to a table of T-shirts and starts refolding them.

I roll my eyes. When your grandma calls you honey it makes you feel special. But when a girl with dangly earrings and red streaked hair calls you that, it makes you feel like a baby.

I dig around in the bin and find a leopard print headband. "Brooke," I say to myself because it looks like something she would wear. I set it off to the side. I dig a little more and find a kitten charm bracelet, which makes me think of Jolene because she loves animals. "And these are for Jenna," I say to myself, picking up a pair of ladybug barrettes.

"She would love to wear bugs in her hair, even if they aren't real."

Then I gasp and pull a pair of ice cream cone earrings from the bin. The same earrings I gave to Stacey for Christmas along with a jumbo box of Choco Chunks. I wrote *Have a Sweet Holiday!* on the tag.

Maybe I should buy this pair for *me*. It's a silly idea because I don't even have pierced ears. Still, I could look at them and think about how they match Stacey's earrings. And how we could match too.

"Can we help you find anything, *honey*?" I hear someone say.

I look up and my mouth drops. "Brooke?" I say. "Stacey?"

Stacey and Brooke hurry up to me.

"What are you doing here?" I ask.

"Duh," Brooke says. "Shopping. And also *this* . . ." She flicks back her long hair. "Ta-da!"

Brooke's earlobes are bright red. I see small diamonds sparkling right above her regular earrings.

"You got your ears double pierced!" I say.

"Genius," Brooke replies.

"I had to come along and hold her hand," Stacey says, giggling.

Brooke giggles too. She clutches Stacey's hand, like a drama queen. "I couldn't have done it without my BFF!"

They practically fall into the jewelry bin, laughing.

I practically fall in too. Not because I'm laughing. Because of what Brooke called Stacey.

BFF.

Best Friend Forever.

I bury the ice cream cone earrings and try to laugh along.

"I'm starved," Brooke says when she comes up for air. "Who wants a cheesy pretzel? My treat." She reaches into her jeans pocket and pulls out two twenty-dollar bills. She glances at the back of the store, where her mom is talking with my mom. "Compliments from my mother's purse," she whispers to us.

Stacey's eyes go wide. "You took it?"

Brooke shrugs. "She told me I could take some money for a treat. It's not my fault she didn't mention how much."

Brooke tucks the bills back into her pocket and squints at me. "You're not going to *tell* on me, are you, Ida?"

"Ida wouldn't tell," Stacey says, looking at me. "Would you?"

"Of course not," I say.

Stacey smiles and turns to Brooke. "See?" she says. "Like I told you. Ida's not a tattletale."

"Except for at school," Brooke says.

My eyes start to sting, so I glance away.

Stacey sees me blinking and quickly grabs Brooke's arm. "Must. Have. Pretzel. Now!" she says, tugging Brooke away from me.

Brooke laughs and glances back. "I suppose you can have one too," she says to me. "As a reward for not tattling *again*."

"Um . . . thanks," I reply. "But I've still got some shopping to do." I pretend to be very interested in a snowflake necklace I pull from the bin.

"What are you shopping for?" Stacey asks.

"New clothes maybe," I reply.

"Oooo," Brooke says. "That's my specialty. I'll help."

"But . . ." I say, thinking about the kind of

159

clothes Brooke might choose for me. The extra-sparkly kind. "I wouldn't want you to starve or anything."

Brooke pulls a pair of sparkly silver earrings from the bin. "Let's start with an accessory," she says, ignoring me. "We'll build the outfit from there. That's a trick I learned from listening to Jade and her friends." Brooke holds the earrings up to a rack of hoodies with lots of sparkles decorating them.

"But Brooke, that's silly," Stacey says. "Remember? Ida can't wear earrings."

Brooke does a dramatic sigh. "Oh, that's right. Ida can't get her ears pierced until she's . . . what? Twenty?"

"Close," I mumble.

Brooke is just about to toss the earrings back into the bin, but then she stops and studies them like a math problem. A moment later her eyes brighten and her mouth curls up at the corners. "Of course," she says to herself. "That's *it*."

"What's it?" Stacey asks.

Brooke tosses the earrings back into the bin and flicks her hair. "Just an idea," she says. "A very excellent idea. But you'll have to wait until Monday to find out!"

Mom looks a little shaky on the drive home. Probably from all the coffee she drank with Brooke's mom while Stacey and Brooke helped me shop at the Mish Mosh.

I'm a little shaky too, only not from coffee. I spent all of my money on a new outfit that I didn't choose. I even had to borrow extra from Mom, which means I couldn't buy any bonus presents for the girls.

"I can't wait to see what you picked out," Mom says as we pull into our driveway.

"Mmm-hmm," I say back.

Dad is on the porch, taking down Christmas lights. He looks up as we get out of the car. "How'd it go?"

I hold up my bag. "Ta-da."

Dad gives me a thumbs-up.

I head into the house.

Dear Stella,
  I saw Stacey and Brooke at the mall today.

They helped me pick out a new outfit. Only
Brooke did most of the picking. That's one of her
talents. I got a bright orange shirt covered with
sparkly X's and O's. A skirt with purple fringe.
Striped leggings. And a pair of clunky black
shoes with big silver buckles. They make me
feel like a pilgrim.

But I don't mind the outfit as much as the
other stuff. Stuff like Stacey and Brooke talking
about the movie they watched last night that
I didn't see. And comparing nail polish that
I'm not wearing. And making jokes that I don't
understand. And, most of all, listening to Brooke
call Stacey "BFF" at least ten times, like it's
her new name or something. And Stacey acting
like it's completely normal for Brooke to be
calling her that.

Brooke is keeping a secret from us until
Monday. That's another one of her talents.
Keeping secrets. Especially when it drives other
people crazy.

Bye,
Ida

Chapter

14

Jenna doesn't notice that I'm wearing a new outfit when I get to the bus stop on Monday morning because she's too busy peeking inside the snack container she's holding. Today is the day we have to bring our shapes snack to school.

Quinn doesn't notice because he's wrestling with his invisible friends again.

Besides, my sparkly shirt and most of my skirt are hidden under my same old jacket. My pilgrim shoes are in my backpack. So really, you can only see my striped leggings.

Rachel studies my legs for a minute. "What happened to your pants?" she asks.

"Yeah, what happened to your pants?" Tess chimes in.

"I'm not wearing any," I say.

Rachel's eyes go wide. "On purpose?"

I nod. "I'm wearing a skirt, see?" I pull up on my jacket so Rachel and Tess can see my purple fringe.

Rachel frowns. "But you always wear pants," she says.

"Not always," I reply. "Sometimes I wear skirts for parties and stuff."

"Are you going to a party?" Tess asks.

I think about the girls meeting to vote on my triple-dog dare today. "Not exactly," I say.

"But what about recess?" Rachel asks. "If you don't got pants to wear, they make you stand by the wall."

Tess nods. "You can't do anything fun by the wall."

"Don't worry," I say. "My snow pants are in my backpack. I won't have to stand by the wall."

Tess and Rachel do big breaths of relief.

Jenna snaps her snack container shut. "Rachel," she says in her big-sister voice. "Stop being a pest."

"I'm not being a pest," Rachel replies. "I'm just being worried about Ida. Like you are being worried about Mommy."

Jenna huffs. "You're crazy."

"No, I am not," Rachel says. "You are always saying worried stuff like, 'Do you feel okay, Mommy?' and 'Do you want some 7UP, Mommy?' and 'Be quiet, Rachel, so Mommy can rest.' *That's* worried stuff."

"Yeah," Tess says. "Worried stuff."

Jenna huffs again and doesn't say anything.

Stacey and Brooke squeal as soon as they see me. They unzip my jacket and pull off my backpack before I even make it to my coat hook.

When they see my sparkly shirt they squeal again.

"Is it picture day?" Randi asks as Brooke hangs up my jacket.

"*Duh*," Jenna says, shifting her snack container. "That was months ago."

"I got a new outfit," I say to Randi.

"That we picked out!" Brooke says, linking arms with Stacey.

"It's perfect," Jolene says, looking me over. "You can borrow my scrunchy, which will make it even perfecter." She pulls a purple scrunchy from her pocket and runs her fingers through my hair like a human hairbrush. It tugs a little, but I don't mind. I'm just happy they're all acting like I'm part of the group again.

Meeka unzips my backpack, yanking out my snow pants and snack container. Then she takes out my pilgrim shoes. She pulls off my snow boots and steers my feet into them.

Randi shakes her head. "We're supposed to be planning Ida's dare, not playing beauty queen."

"Later," Brooke says. "Beauty can't wait." She snorts a laugh. So do the others. So do I.

When the bell rings they start to parade me into our classroom, but I pull back. "I have to get my shapes snack," I say. "And hang up my stuff."

"Well, hurry," Brooke says. "We want to show the new you to Mr. Crow."

Everyone heads inside without me. I hang my snow pants on my coat hook and shove my boots out of the way.

"You don't like it, do you?" I hear someone say.

I look up and see Jenna watching me from our classroom doorway.

"Don't like what?" I ask.

"You know what," she says. "Why did you let them pick out clothes you don't want?"

I look down at my sparkly shirt, purple fringed skirt, and stripped leggings. I shift in my clunky black shoes. "I just thought if I let them choose the outfit, maybe they would forget about choosing a triple-dog dare."

Jenna huffs. "Like that would ever happen. Brooke lives for this stuff. Don't you know?"

I do know.

I shift some more.

Jenna turns and walks into the classroom.

I clunk along behind.

Everyone is huddled around Mr. Crow's desk comparing the snacks they brought.

"I've got cheese cubes," Meeka says, holding up a zipper bag of small yellow and white cubes.

"I brought saltines for squares," Zane adds.

"Cheese and crackers," Mr. Crow says, leaning back in his chair. "One of my favorite snacks."

Stacey and Brooke show the cookies they baked. "They're round, like circles," Stacey says.

"Plus, they have M&M'S, which are also

round," Brooke says. "So we should definitely get extra credit."

Mr. Crow just smiles.

Quinn opens the lid on his container, but I don't see what's inside it because someone starts tapping my shoulder.

I turn and see Randi's bright green eyes. "It's all set," she whispers. "We're gonna meet during morning recess to vote on your triple-dog dare!"

"Oh, boy," I whisper back. "Where do we meet?"

"Not you," Randi says. "Just *us*." She glances around at the other girls. "We'll tell you all about it this afternoon."

"I searched through three bags of corn chips to find enough perfect triangles," Joey says, holding up a clear plastic bag of chips. "It was grueling."

"What did you do with the ones that weren't perfect?" Tom asks. "Wait, let me guess. Ate them, right?"

Joey rubs his stomach and smiles. Then he burps.

"I brought grapes," Jolene says. "For spheres."

Jenna huffs. "You *always* bring grapes, Jolene."

That's true. Jolene is the grape girl in our class.

"Grapes are a good choice," Mr. Crow says. "Healthy *and* spherical. A perfectly shaped snack."

Jolene gives Jenna a squint.

"What did you bring, Ida?" Mr. Crow asks.

"Um . . . Jell-O," I say.

"*Jell-O?*" Jenna says. "That doesn't have a shape. It's just a blob."

"It's *finger* Jell-O," I say. I lift the lid on my container and show everyone the jiggly red hexagons inside.

"Yum!" Stacey says.

"Very creative!" Mr. Crow adds.

"That's nothing," Jenna says. "I got stars, and hardly any snacks come in that shape."

"Actually," Tom says, "if you cut an apple in half sideways, you'll find a star inside."

Jenna squints. "This isn't kindergarten, Tom."

"So what did you bring?" Dominic asks.

Jenna lifts her chin. "It's very rare. I had to make my dad drive to three grocery stores before we found any."

Everyone crowds closer to Jenna. She soaks us up like a sponge. Then she slowly raises the lid on her snack container like she's opening an Egyptian tomb. Slices of star-shaped fruit are inside. Four rows with four stars each. Sixteen stars altogether.

"Ah, star fruit," Mr. Crow says. "That's also very creative, Jenna."

Jenna nods.

"I've never had star fruit before," Jolene says, nudging in for a closer look. "What does it taste like?"

"Like grapes," I mumble.

Jenna snaps the lid shut on her container, just missing Jolene's nose. "*No* samples," she says. "You have to wait until snack time like everyone else."

Jenna pushes past us. She sits down at her desk and recounts her stars.

Since I'm not allowed to be around when the girls vote on my triple-dog dare, I volunteer to fix up a snack table for Mr. Crow during our morning recess. But as soon as everyone starts coming back inside I leave the snacks and find Stacey.

"What did you decide?" I ask her.

"We decided Brooke had the best idea ever!" Stacey says. "You are going to love this dare!"

"Love a triple-dog dare?" I say. "But they're supposed to make you smell bad. Or lose your hair. Or get you grounded for a month."

Stacey giggles. "Not this one. You'll see, this afternoon!"

"Can't you tell me now?"

"Sorry," Stacey says, pretending to lock her lips with an invisible key. "I'm sworn to secrecy until our next recess."

"But I'm your best friend," I remind her. "You're supposed to tell me secrets."

"If I told you, everyone would be mad at me," Stacey says.

"Yes, but *I* would be happy with you," I reply.

Stacey thinks for a minute. "Okay, I'll give you a hint, but that's all." She pulls me off to the side and huddles in close. "Your dare is something you have been wanting to do, but can't. That's why you'll love it!"

"But there are lots of things I've been wanting to do, but can't. Cartwheels, for example. Straight A's on my report card. Burping the alphabet." I give Stacey a very pleading look. "Can't you give me a better hint?"

"Nope," Stacey says. "You'll just have to wait."

I sigh because waiting is something else I can't do so great.

It's a hot day because of my stripped leggings. And itchy, because of my sparkly shirt. I concentrate on not scratching so the sparkles won't get on my hands and end up on my chin or on my nose or on some other part of me where you don't normally wear sparkles.

All the concentrating makes my brain tired, so I rest it on my desk during free time. All I can smell is eraser shavings. All I can see is Tom's right arm.

I count the lint balls on his sleeve.

Twenty-seven.

Then I close my eyes and try to imagine what my triple-dog dare will be. And how I could ever love it.

I'm in the middle of imagining the girls daring me to eat a jumbo box of Choco Chunks, which is the only dare I could ever love, when a sheet of paper slides onto my desk. A drawing, actually. It looks like one of the pictures from Tom's Picasso art book. Like a boy—Tom, maybe—made out of triangles, squares, and circles instead of bones, skin, and sneakers.

"It's a *get-well* picture," Tom whispers.

I glance at him and notice that his ears are bright red, just like the tiny heart he drew on the boy's square chest.

"Thanks," I whisper back. "But I'm not actually sick. Just a little . . . itchy."

"Oh," Tom replies, shifting in his seat. "Then I guess it's a . . . *itch-well* picture."

"Neat," I say. "Can I keep it?"

"That was the plan," he says.

I smile and put the drawing inside my desk. Then I rest my head again.

Just before our second recess, Mr. Crow sends me to the nurse so she can check my temperature.

It's the only thing about me that's normal today.

Chapter
15

I get back from the nurse's office in plenty of time for recess.

In a few minutes, I'll know what my dare is.

And how much I will love it.

I wait with Stacey outside the snow fort while the other girls get situated inside. Brooke wants to make the whole thing very dramatic.

She waves and we step inside the snow fort. "Stacey, please present the accused."

I gulp.

Stacey takes my arm and clears her throat. "I present . . . Ida May," she says, all official.

Everyone giggles. Except for Jenna. Her face is like a blank page in my sketchbook.

We sit down and Brooke gives Meeka and Jolene a nod.

They scramble up and start dancing. It's a small dance because there's not a lot of room. And short because they're making it up as they go.

Everyone thumps their mittens together as Meeka and Jolene take a bow.

"You next, Randi," Brooke says.

Randi scoops up a fistful of snow and stands over me. "Ida May," she says, "it's time to announce the charges against you." She sprinkles snow on my head. I don't ask why. "You are accused of spilling the beans on your friends," Randi continues. "Any last words?"

I brush snowflakes off my eyelashes. "Um . . . I'm sorry I did it," I say. "Please don't make me eat a bug."

Everyone giggles. Even Jenna lets some slip.

Randi steps back.

Brooke takes center stage. "And now," she says, brushing away the hair that's stuck to her lip gloss, "by the powers invented in me, I hereby announce your triple-dog dare!"

Everyone squirms and whispers. Kids laugh and shout in the distance. Snowflakes fall from the blue-gray sky. One lands on my coat sleeve.

I can see its six perfect points. I think about all the snowflakes piled up around me and how this one is different from all of them. And how much sky it had to drift through before it landed on me.

Brooke straightens her snow pants. "Ida May, we dare you to—" She pauses to clear her throat. "To—"

"Let Meeka pierce your ears!" Jolene blurts out.

Brooke shoots a look at Jolene. "I was supposed to say that!"

Jolene covers her mouth with her fuzzy white mittens. "Oops."

My eyes go wide. "Um . . . could you repeat that, please?"

"Yes," Brooke says. "We dare you to let Meeka pierce your ears!"

I blink at Meeka.

Meeka nods. "If I'm going to be a doctor someday, I need to practice poking people with needles." She bites off her glove and reaches inside her coat pocket. She pulls out a pencil and flips open a little notebook. "How does tomorrow work for you?" She holds her pencil over the notebook and glances up at me. "Say, fourish?"

"Um . . . not so great," I say, trying to think of a reason why I can't get my ears pierced tomorrow. Then I remember one. "I have to walk Rachel to her piano lesson after school tomorrow. It's a very important job."

I glance at Jenna, hoping she won't offer to walk Rachel for me. My stomach loosens a little when Jenna glances away.

Meeka flips to another page in her notebook. "I'm completely booked on Wednesday," she says. "How about Thursday?"

"We have dance on Thursday, remember?" Stacey says.

Meeka nods and jots a note. "I have an opening on Friday, after school." She taps the pencil against her chin. "That would give you the weekend to recover."

"Sounds . . . perfect," I say.

"Oooo . . ." Brooke says. "That gives me the best idea!"

We all wait for Brooke to fill us in.

"I'll have a sleep-over at my house on Friday

night and Meeka can pierce Ida's ears then!" Brooke says. "We'll make it a real ceremony!"

"*Dare*mony is more like it," Randi says.

"Yeah, a *dare*mony!" Jolene says. "Meeka and me will do another dance. Only we'll practice this time."

Meeka nods.

"And Stacey can help me decorate," Brooke says, smiling at Stacey.

"Will do!" Stacey replies.

"What about me?" Randi says. "I need a job."

"You can bring the potato," Brooke says. "We'll need one to hold it behind Ida's ear so Meeka doesn't poke her head."

"Potato patrol," Randi says. "Roger."

Brooke starts explaining all about piercing ears because she overheard Jade's friend Meghan tell how she pierced her cousin's ears for her.

Meeka takes lots of notes.

Everyone is acting like the daremony is Brooke's best idea ever.

Everyone except Jenna.

Everyone except me.

"Um . . . excuse me," I say when Brooke stops

to take a breath. "I hate to interrupt, but there's one, tiny problem."

"What?" they all ask.

"My parents won't let me get my ears pierced until I'm ten."

"So?" Brooke says. "Just hide your ears until your next birthday."

"*Hide* my ears?"

Brooke nods. "Scarves, hoodies, hats. Problem solved."

"You can borrow my earmuffs," Stacey says. "They'll hide your ears *and* keep you nice and toasty." She tosses her fuzzy purple earmuffs onto my lap and gives me a warm smile. "You can start wearing them now for practice."

"But my birthday isn't until *summer*," I say. "I can't wear earmuffs until—"

"It's all settled then," Brooke cuts in. "Daremony at my house Friday night. Be there or be square."

Everyone gets up and starts heading back inside.

I pull off my hat and put on Stacey's earmuffs.

I lean against the snow fort and think about how sweaty my life is going to be.

Dear Stella,
    I got my triple-dog dare today. I have to let Meeka pierce my ears at Brooke's sleep-over on Friday. I would almost rather kiss a cane toad. Or maybe even a boy. How could Stacey think I would love this dare? I even asked her how she could think that during silent reading. She said, "Getting your ears pierced is fun!" and I said, "Not if Meeka is piercing them" and she said, "It's easy and there's hardly any blood" and I said, "Blood?!" and she said, "Won't it be fun to swap earrings?" and I said, "How much blood?" and then Mr. Crow said, "Shhh! This is <u>silent</u> reading, girls. Save the chatter for later."
    Later we watched a slideshow about Pablo Picasso. Tom had shown Mr. Crow his book and got him all inspired. We even had to draw ourselves using shapes like Mr. Picasso did. Circles, triangles, squares. I chose scribbles because that's how I've been feeling lately and

Mr. Picasso's drawings are all about feelings.

Jenna looked over at my drawing and said, "A scribble is not a shape."

Then Tom looked at Jenna and said, "A friend is not a boss."

Then Quinn looked at all of us and said, "A booger is not a snack."

That made us laugh. Even Jenna.

Mr. Crow must have been feeling especially creative, because we hardly got a break before he started teaching us about concrete poems, which are poems that are shaped like the thing you're writing about. So, if your poem is about a triangle, it's shaped like a triangle. If it's about a tiger, it's shaped like a tiger.

For homework we have to write a concrete poem using an easy shape. Here's mine:

**one
big yellow
circle in the sky
grows apples
for making
pie**

I signed my name like this:

Which is how I would look if I were a poem.

Chapter

16

I tried calling Stacey last night to talk about the daremony, but her grandma told me a friend invited her to the Purdee Good for ice cream.

I bet I know which friend.

And now I won't have time to talk to her before school because my dad has the morning off, so he's taking me out for breakfast.

"Everything good?" Dad asks as we head to the Purdee Good. "I mean with school and everything?"

"Yep," I say.

Dad glances at me and then back at the road. "Anything bad?"

"Nope."

I watch snowbanks rise and fall outside my window.

"I hear you're walking Rachel home after her piano lessons."

"Mmm-hmm," I say.

"That's a big help to Mom."

I nod.

"And to Mrs. Drews," Dad continues. "Especially considering . . . everything."

Dad turns on his blinker and we head down Main Street.

"Everything? You mean about Mr. Drews's job? Because he got a new one. Jenna said so."

Dad nods and waves to someone walking down the snowy sidewalk. "That, and Mrs. Drews's not feeling well lately."

"I know, but Jenna said it's only temporary."

"Mmm-hmm," Dad says. "A baby can do that. I know Mom felt queasy when she was expecting you."

Dad slows down suddenly as a couple of kids run across the street in front of us. I jerk forward and my seat belt snaps to attention.

So do I.

"Baby?" I say. "What baby?"

Dad glances at me. "Mrs. Drews's baby. She's expecting. Didn't Jenna tell you?"

184

I sit back. "Nope," I say.

"Huh," Dad says. "Mom didn't mention that it's a secret." He parks next to the Purdee Good and turns off the car. "Better keep it under your hat . . . er . . . earmuffs for now, okay?"

"Okay," I say.

I watch Jenna out of the corner of my eye all day at school. I wonder why she hasn't mentioned her new baby. I wonder why Rachel hasn't either.

Whenever I'm around Jenna, I drop a few hints.

"Did you see that special on *baby* penguins last night?"

"I just love *baby* carrots, don't you?"

"Tom told me his *baby* sister got a crayon stuck up her nose."

But Jenna doesn't budge.

I think about telling Stacey that Jenna has a big secret.

But if I do, she will probably tell Brooke.

I keep it to myself.

ഐ

When the bus gets to my stop after school, me and Rachel head to my house.

Jenna follows along. Even after we turn the corner.

I stop and look at her. "Um . . . aren't you going the wrong way?"

"Yes," she says. "I mean . . . no. I'm going with you."

"You are?" I say.

"You are?" Rachel says.

Jenna gives us a quick nod. "My mom . . . she told me I should."

Jenna glances away.

"But I don't mind walking Rachel home," I say.

"Yeah, Ida doesn't mind," Rachel chimes in.

Jenna doesn't say anything. She just kicks at a chunk of ice on the sidewalk until she kicks it loose.

"But, I suppose if you want to—" I start to say.

I hear a small cough and look at Rachel. She shakes her head *no*.

I look at Jenna again. "You can walk Rachel home," I say. "Just for today."

Rachel puffs.

Jenna sniffs, shaking back her braids. "If I have to," she says.

I take off for my house.

Rachel catches up.

Jenna follows along.

When we get there we ditch our coats and kick off our boots. I leave Jenna sitting on the staircase while Rachel starts her piano lesson. When I come back from the kitchen with a plate of brownies, Jenna's checking her watch and tapping her foot to "Three Blind Mice." There's a hole in her sock and one toe peeks out. It's painted orange to match her fingernails.

"If you want," I say, "we can wait in my room until Rachel's done."

Jenna's foot skips a beat. She checks her watch again. "I guess that would be okay," she says.

We grab our backpacks and head upstairs.

When we get to my room, Jenna sets her stuff by my bed and walks over to my fish tank. "Is this your new fish?" she asks, tapping on the glass.

I set the brownies on my desk. "Good guess," I say.

My fish darts behind the pirate. "Not very

friendly, is he?" Jenna taps on the glass harder.

"He's just a little shy around strangers," I say.

"We had a fish once," Jenna says. "Two, actually. We won them at a fair."

"What happened to them?" I ask.

Jenna shrugs. "Died. Flushed." She darts her eyes at me. "It was Rachel's fault. She never fed them."

I walk over to the tank and sprinkle fish food onto the water. "I've heard that can be bad for a fish."

My fish darts back and forth, chasing the sinking flakes.

"Wow, look at him go!" Jenna says. "You should name him Zippy."

"*Zippy?*" I say.

Jenna nibbles on the end of her braid. "Well, maybe not Zippy, exactly. That's just short for something better. Like . . . *Zippo*potamus."

"Tom said I should just ask my fish what he wants his name to be."

Jenna snorts. "And everyone thinks he's such a brain."

I shrug. "It's worth a try."

I tap on the fish tank. "Hello, fish," I say. "I was

just wondering what you want your name to be."

Jenna rolls her eyes.

I lean over the top of the tank and cup my hair behind my ear. My fish swims to the surface and nips at a flake.

Jenna moves in closer. "What's he saying?"

"Just *pic, pic, pic* . . ." I reply.

"That's not a name," Jenna says. "Not unless it's short for something like . . . Pickles or . . . Piccolo."

"Or Picasso," I say.

"That's it," Jenna says. "Picasso. Pic for short."

I look into the tank again. "Pic?" I say to my fish. "Is that your name?"

"Of course it is," Jenna says. "Just look at him. He's a mess of colors and shapes like the old guy's paintings."

"Pic . . . pic . . . pic!" my fish says.

I give Jenna a smile. "You're right," I say.

Jenna nods. Then she flicks back her braids and heads for my bed. "We should do our homework now," she says, unzipping her backpack. "Concrete poems?"

"Good plan," I say.

Jenna pulls out a notebook. "You should write one about your new fish," she says. "And I'll write one about my new—"

Jenna presses her lips together.

"New what?" I ask, grabbing the brownies and walking over to her.

"My new . . . dog," she says. "Biscuit." She opens her notebook and grabs the box of oil pastels from my nightstand. She takes out a brown stick and starts doodling a square dog.

I frown. "You've had Biscuit for more than a year. That's not new."

Jenna gives the square dog triangle ears. She doesn't answer.

I take a big, brave breath. "What about your new . . . baby?" I say quietly. "You could write a poem about that."

Jenna stops doodling. She looks up at me.

"How did you know?" she asks.

"My dad told me," I say, sitting down on my bed. "This morning." I take a brownie and set the plate between us. "He didn't know it was a secret." I take a bite. "*Is* it a secret?"

Jenna takes a blue stick out of the box. "Sort

of," she says. "I'm not supposed to tell anyone yet. Especially not Rachel." She draws a circle near the dog—a ball maybe—and fills it in blue.

"Why not?"

"Because sometimes babies don't . . . stick . . . for my mom," she says. "She wants to be sure this one does before Rachel knows about it. She didn't even want me to know, but I overheard her on the phone with her doctor, so I made her spill the beans."

Jenna turns to a clean page in her notebook. "Let's get started."

I set my brownie down and pull my backpack toward me. I take out my notebook and turn to a clean page too.

"Maybe they'll let you pick a name for it," I say. "The baby, I mean."

"Maybe," Jenna says.

"Not Zippy, though," I say.

Jenna picks up a brownie and takes a bite. "Good plan."

Chapter

17

I wait until Thursday morning to ask Mom if I can go to Brooke's sleep-over on Friday night.

Mom laughs. "No way," she says, setting a bowl of oatmeal in front of me at our kitchen table. "Not unless you get your chores done, starting with that *fish*. We made a deal last week, remember? You were supposed to change the filter before we went shopping, but you didn't, did you?"

"Fine," I say. "I'll clean the filter as soon as I get home from school. I mean, as soon as I get home from the Purdee Good. It's cookie day with Stacey." I pick up my spoon and stir the lumps in my oatmeal. "Sugar, please?"

Mom snatches up the sugar container. Then she takes my bowl of oatmeal. "Change the fil-tcr," she says. "*Then* eat. Then I'll drive you to school."

"But—"

"*Now.*"

I slide off my chair and trudge to my room.

Touching the fish filter is the worst thing ever. Even worse than touching Dylan Anderson's shoe. Not that I have, but still.

"How can you live like this?" I ask my fish as I pull the dirty filter out. It looks like something you would step on in a swamp. It smells like it too.

I drop the filter into a bucket.

I slide a new filter into place and plug in the motor again. Water gurgles. My fish swims in happy circles. The pirate lifts his jug.

"If you changed it more often, it wouldn't be so gross," Mom says from my bedroom doorway.

I pick up the bucket. "Can I go to Brooke's sleep-over now?"

"Yes," Mom says. "And after you throw away the old filter and wash your hands, you can have your oatmeal."

I look into the bucket. "Maybe just toast," I say, and head for the garbage.

The bell is ringing when I get to school, so I hurry to hang up my stuff and join everyone else inside our classroom.

I slip my concrete poem into the homework basket on Mr. Crow's desk. I drew a fish shape and wrote my poem inside it. Jenna was there. She said, "The fish could be better, but you rhymed the poem good."

Then I take the long way around the desk square so I can walk past Stacey.

"I get to go to Brooke's sleep-over tomorrow," I whisper to her.

"Good!" Stacey whispers back.

I do a half smile. "Are we going to the Purdee Good after dance today?" I ask.

"Of course," Stacey says. "Like always."

This time I do a whole smile.

All day long it's sleep-over this and sleep-over that. The more Brooke and the other girls talk about it, the more I pinch my earlobes. My fingernails are sharp enough to leave dents in them. But they're not as sharp as needles.

Brooke says I won't feel a thing when Meeka

pierces my ears because they will freeze them with ice first. But I'm not so sure. I kept my ears uncovered for our whole afternoon recess. They were red and stinging when I got back inside. But when I pressed my fingernails into them I could still feel the pinch.

There are only a couple of people in the Purdee Good when I get there after walking Stacey to Miss Woo's after school. I scoot onto a stool by the counter and slip off my backpack. I unzip my jacket and pull off my mittens and earmuffs.

"Those look just like Stacey's earmuffs," Kelli says as she sets a glass of milk in front of me.

"They are Stacey's," I reply. "We swapped for a while."

Kelli smiles. "My best friend Barb and I used to swap stuff all the time when we were kids. Hats. Clothes. Shoes. We were exactly the same size until eighth grade."

"Then what happened?"

"Then Barb grew up and I grew . . . out." Kelli does a little laugh.

"Did you stay best friends?"

"No, not really," she says. "We were still friends, just not best friends. In high school, Barb was into sports and I was into books and—well—boys." Kelli looks past me, thinking. "We sort of . . . drifted."

I take a sip of milk.

Kelli clears away a couple of coffee cups. "Cookie?" she asks.

"No thanks," I say. "I'll wait until Stacey gets here."

Kelli sets the dirty cups in a plastic bin and starts wiping the counter with a damp rag. She hums while she works and her earrings sparkle under the warm café lights. I study them for a minute.

"Did it hurt?" I ask.

Kelli glances at me. "Did what hurt?"

"Getting your ears pierced."

Kelli stops wiping. "Yes," she says. "A little."

I nod. "That's what I thought."

Kelli walks over to me and leans against the counter. "Are you thinking about getting your ears pierced, Ida?" she asks.

"A little," I say.

Kelli tosses the rag into the bin with the dirty

cups and looks at me again. "If you're worried about it, I'm sure Stacey would go with you. In fact, she just went with Brooke to that piercing boutique at the mall, so she's all practiced up."

I nod again and sip my milk.

Kelli smiles. "That's what best friends are for, right? To hold your hand through the tough stuff?"

"I guess," I say.

A couple of people come into the café and Kelli gets busy with her job again. I take my milk to one of the booths and watch snowflakes fall outside the big café window. The streetlights blink on, making patches of the sidewalk look warm and golden. But it's still cold and gray around the edges.

Stacey and the other girls come out of Miss Woo's. They laugh and throw snow and shout good-bye to each other. Brooke, Meeka, and Jolene climb into cars and drive away. Jenna walks down the sidewalk by herself. Stacey waits for the street to clear and then crosses over to me.

The door jingles. "Hi!" Stacey sings. She hangs up her stuff on the coat tree.

"Hi, Stace," Kelli says, leaning across the counter to give her a kiss. "How was dance?"

"Good," she says, scooting in across from me. "We started working on our dance for the spring recital. It's pretty hard, but Brooke and I are going to practice on the weekends when I don't have to go to Dad's."

Kelli brings Stacey a glass of milk and sets a giant cookie between us.

"You and Brooke?" Kelli says.

Stacey nods and breaks the cookie in half. "We get to do a duet. It's going to be the best part of the whole recital!"

Stacey eats her half of the cookie and tells me all about the dance they're going to do, and how she hopes their recital costumes will be purple and sparkly, and how Miss Woo told her she was born to be a dancer and that she and Brooke are a perfect match for the duet.

I nod and smile while she talks.

But on the inside I'm thinking about best friends and how they don't always match. Like Brooke and Jenna. They were best friends until this year. Now they are best enemies. And me and Stacey. We're best friends, I know we are. But now she's Brooke's best friend too. Maybe Brooke matches her better than me.

Dear Stella,

    Mr. Crow liked my concrete poem so much he hung it up on the board in our classroom today. Actually, he hung up everyone's poems, but still, mine was pretty good. I even have it memorized:

> My Fish by Ida May
> Diving!
> Dipping! Fins flipping!
> Scales bright. Black, orange,
> White. Watch him go—
> My fish, Picasso.

    Jenna's poem was the shortest one. She wrote it in a circle. The hollow kind:

circling for a friend. Circling, circling start to end. Circling, circling.

She must have been feeling sad when she wrote it because of fighting with Brooke and because of keeping the secret about her new baby. That's probably why she used my blue oil pastel stick. Because blue can be a sad color. Like that sad guitar player Mr. Picasso drew.

And the circle makes me think of the way birds fly around and around when they're looking for someplace to land or for something to eat. Only in the poem, Jenna isn't looking for a tree branch or a bug.

Bye,
Ida

Chapter

18

My dad drives me to Brooke's house for the sleep-over.

"Have fun!" he says as we pull up to her house.

"I'll try," I say, reaching for my stuff.

"Everything okay?" Dad asks.

I shrug. "Sure," I say. "Everything's fine."

"You just seem a little down lately. Did you and Stacey have a fight?"

"No," I say. "We're fine too."

A car pulls up in front of us. Meeka and Jolene pile out and run up the steps to Brooke's front door. Meeka's dad turns and waves to us before driving away.

"Do you want to skip this one?" Dad asks. "There'll be other sleep-overs."

I think about how easy it would be to skip

it. And how hard. If I don't go, everyone will be mad at me all over again. And I'd still have to do a triple-dog dare some other time. Maybe a worse one. Although getting poked with a needle sounds like the worst one to me.

I glance at Dad. "I'll be okay."

Dad gives me half a smile. Then he leans over and gives me a hug. "Easy on the soda," he whispers in my ear. "And watch out for toothpaste on the toilet seat."

"I will," I say.

I hug him back a little longer than usual.

I climb out of the car and get my sleeping bag from the backseat.

"Bye," I say.

"Bye, Ida," Dad replies. "Have fun."

I close the door.

Stacey opens Brooke's front door when I ring the bell.

"Ida!" she sings. "You're here!"

"Yep," I say. "You too."

"I've been here *forever*!" Stacey says, all breathless. "Brooke made me come early to help make the pagoda."

"The what?"

"The pagoda," Stacey says, pulling me inside and closing the door. "It's like a tent. We hung sheets over chairs and strung up Christmas lights. Meeka will pierce your ears inside it!"

"A piercing pagoda," I say.

"Exactly," Stacey says back. "C'mon! The party's this way!" She takes my stuff and heads for the staircase.

I toss my jacket onto a pile of others that are spilling off a bench. Stacey's, Randi's, Meeka's, and Jolene's.

Stacey stops on the stairs and turns halfway back to me. "Did you notice?" she asks, fluttering her eyelids.

"Is that . . . mascara?" I study Stacey's clumpy eyelashes. "And eyeliner?"

Stacey nods. "Jade did it. She even did Randi! Wait 'til you see. She's going to do everyone's makeup as long as we don't bug her all night."

Stacey starts up the stairs again and I follow along, remembering that Brooke's parents are at a dinner tonight. They called to let my mom and dad know that Jade's in charge until they get home.

I've been to Brooke's house a couple of times for birthday parties, but this is the first time I've been upstairs. Stacey leads me down a long hallway. The floor is covered with squishy pink carpet. It's like walking on a tongue. The walls are covered with pictures of Jade and Brooke. A door is open at the far end of the hallway. Music pours out of it. Some boy band. I see Randi sifting through a stack of CDs. Brooke, Meeka, and Jolene are tossing pillows into a pagoda.

"Don't use this bathroom," Stacey says as we walk past a closed door. "Brooke's mom is having it redecorated."

The next door we walk past is closed too. Music booms from behind it. Big, hollow notes that pound against my chest. It sounds like the stuff my dad listens to when my mom's not home. A poster is tacked to the door. It has a picture of a lady wearing an old-fashioned cape over a long dress. Her dark hair is pulled up under a tall hat that looks like an upside-down bucket. She's holding a cane. Or maybe it's a whip. Next to her it says, *I do not want people to be very agreeable as it saves me the trouble of liking them a great deal.* Jane Austen.

"Jade's room," Stacey says, glancing at the poster. "Don't go in there either."

Brooke pokes her head out from the room at the end of the hall. "There you are!" she says to Stacey. "I thought you got lost!"

"Ida's here!" Stacey says. "I'm giving her the tour."

"Well, hurry up. We still have a ton of stuff to do."

Brooke ducks back inside her bedroom. The music coming from Jade's room fades a little and I hear chimes.

"Doorbell!" Stacey says.

"I'll get it," I offer. "Brooke needs you."

"Thanks," Stacey says. She hurries down the hallway to Brooke's room. I head downstairs.

I pull open the front door. Jenna is standing on the other side.

"You're here!" I say, trying to sound as sparkly as Stacey.

"Why wouldn't I be?" Jenna says back. "I did get invited, you know."

"I know," I say, stepping aside.

Jenna walks in and I take her stuff.

"You can leave your coat there," I say, nodding toward the bench. "Then I'll show you the way."

"I know the way," Jenna says, dumping her coat. "I practically lived here when Brooke and I were best friends."

Jenna trudges up the stairs.

I rearrange her stuff in my arms and trudge up too.

At first, everything is just like an ordinary sleep-over. We bounce on Brooke's bed, eat junk food, and laugh while Randi lip-syncs to songs in her glittery makeup and camo clothes. We even sneak down the hall to Jade's room and press our ears against her door, biting back giggles.

"What's she doing in there?" Jolene whispers.

"Who knows," Brooke whispers back. "Just don't let her catch you sneak—"

Jade's door flies open. We all stumble back.

Jade glares at us. "*What.*" She doesn't say it like a question.

Brooke steps up. "We just wanted to tell you that everyone is here," she says. "Can you finish doing our makeup now?"

Jade flips her cell phone shut. She slips it into the front pocket of her jeans. Then she steps out of her room and pulls the door closed behind her.

She turns to Brooke. "No," she says.

Brooke crosses her arms and scowls as we watch Jade disappear down the stairs.

"Great," Brooke grumbles. "She's in a mood. We better not bug her again until my mom and dad get home. Then she'll have to be nice to us."

"What should we do until then?" Meeka asks.

"What we came here for," Randi says. "The daremony!"

Everyone looks at me.

"So soon?" I say.

Brooke's mouth curls into a grin. "Randi?" she says. "Got the potato?"

"Check!" Randi says back.

"Meeka? Needles?"

"Check check!" Meeka says.

Brooke nods. "I'll get the ice. The rest of you clean up the pagoda. We need a completely sterile environment. Five minutes!"

Brooke takes off for the stairs. Everyone else heads to Brooke's room.

Randi runs to her backpack and digs out a potato. "Here, Ida," she says. "Hold this behind your ear so Meeka doesn't poke your brain out."

Randi tosses the potato to me, but I miss. It bounces on the carpet and rolls to Meeka's feet. "Time for your pre-op exam," she says to me.

I pick up the potato. "I have to take a quiz?"

Meeka pulls me aside while the other girls fuss with the pagoda. "Exam," she says, squeezing my right earlobe. "As in *examination*?" She squeezes my left earlobe and frowns. "Hmm . . . thicker than I thought."

"Is that . . . bad?" I ask.

Meeka steps back and studies my ears for a moment. Then she pulls a pincushion out of her sleep-over bag. It's tomato-shaped and prickly with pins and needles. "This should do it," she says, pulling out the longest needle I've ever seen.

I gulp and look around for Stacey. But she's with the others, inside the pagoda.

"I'm back," Brooke says, running into the room with a cup of ice. She closes the door and leans against it, breathing hard. "Ohmygosh, that was so close!"

Everyone peeks out of the pagoda. "What happened?" Jolene asks.

"Jade saw me getting ice and was all, *'No soda upstairs'* and so I had to think super fast and say, 'It's not for soda. It's for Randi. She twisted her ankle in PE.'"

"Good thinking!" Stacey says.

"I know," Brooke replies. She looks at Randi. "Be sure to limp if you see Jade."

"Got it," Randi says.

Brooke jiggles her cup and the ice cubes clink inside. "Let the daremony begin!"

"What about our dance?" Jolene says, crawling out of the pagoda. "Meeka and I practiced for hours."

"Fine," Brooke says. "Do your dance, but hurry before my ice melts."

Meeka sets the pincushion on Brooke's desk and grabs her bag. She and Jolene whisper some instructions to Brooke, then disappear into the hallway. The rest of us—me and Stacey, Randi and Jenna—climb onto Brooke's bed.

"Ready?" Brooke asks.

"Ready!" we all reply.

Brooke pops a CD into her player. Creepy music slithers out. The kind you hear during a scary scene in a movie. She shuts off the lights and unplugs the pagoda. It's totally dark and we can't help but fake-scream.

Brooke dives onto the bed. We bounce like crazy and I nearly drop my potato. "Shhh!" Brooke says, crawling out of our tangled arms and legs. "Here they come!"

Meeka and Jolene step into the room and close the door. They're wearing black sweatshirts now, with the hoods up, and holding flashlights under their chins. They blink them off and on so their faces glow like zombies.

"Spooky!" Randi says.

Meeka and Jolene start dancing in a very zombie-ish way and I scoot closer to Stacey because sometimes it feels safer to sit extra-close to your best friend.

I nudge Stacey's arm. "Creepy, huh?"

"I've seen creepier."

I look at Stacey. Only it's not her. It's Jenna.

"Oh," I say. "Sorry. I thought you were Stacey."

"No, it's just me," Jenna says. "Stacey bounced over there." Jenna points to the foot of the bed, where Brooke and Stacey are huddled together, sucking on ice cubes and squealing every time Meeka and Jolene snatch at them with their zombie hands.

"We should play ghost in the graveyard after this," Randi says. She swings her arm like a pendulum. "One o'clock, two o'clock, three o'clock . . ."

"No games until after the daremony," Brooke says. She slides off the bed and switches on the lights.

"Hey, we weren't finished yet!" Meeka says.

"Sorry," Brooke replies. "But my ice is having a serious melt-down. We can't wait any longer."

"I don't mind waiting," I say. "Really."

"Meeka, get your needles," Brooke says. "Ida, bring the potato. Everyone, into the pagoda. *Now!*"

Everyone does what Brooke says.

Except me.

I just sit on the bed thinking about how much I don't want to do this. "Wait," I say. But no one hears me because they are talking and laughing and crawling over each other to get to the pagoda.

I drop my potato on the bed and stand up. I plant my feet in the squishy carpet and breathe in as much air as my lungs will hold. *"Waaaait!"* I shout as loudly as I can. Which, as it turns out, is pretty loud.

Everyone freezes.

"Now what?" Brooke says.

"I need . . . I need . . . to go to the bathroom," I say.

Brooke groans and sits back on her heels. "Well, hurry up!" she says. "I am *not* getting more ice. If Jade catches me she will start asking questions."

"But, I don't know where it is," I say. "The bathroom, I mean."

Brooke groans again and starts to stand. "Downstairs and to the right," she says. "I'll show you."

But I don't want Brooke to go with me. I want my best friend to.

I look straight at Stacey. Straight *through* her. I mouth the word *please.*

Stacey does a puzzled look. Then her face goes smooth. She grabs my arm. "Be right back," she says to Brooke.

We run out of Brooke's room, down the stairs, slip into the bathroom, and lock the door.

It's a big bathroom, so there's lots of room for me to pace. Stacey leans against the sink. "What's going on?" she asks.

I glance at her and catch my reflection slipping in and out of the big mirror that hangs behind her. "Um . . . it's just . . ." I start to say. "It's not that I don't want to do it . . . but . . . the thing is . . ."

"Ida, what is it?" Stacey pulls me to a stop.

I look at the mirror again and see both of us reflected in it side by side.

I turn and look at the real Stacey. "I—I'm . . . chicken," I say. "I want to get my ears pierced. Really. But not like this. Not with ice. Not with a potato. Not with Meeka poking the needle."

Tears fill my eyes. They tip over my eyelashes and stream down my face. I don't try to stop them.

Crumpling to the floor, I pull my knees up to

my chest, wrap my arms around them, and bury my face.

Then I bawl like the biggest baby in the world.

Stacey crouches next to me. She puts her arm across my shoulders and lets me cry.

"It's okay," Stacey says. "Don't worry. I'll fix it."

Chapter

19

After I finish crying and splash water on my face and blow my nose three times and let Stacey try to hide my puffy eyelids behind my bangs, we head back to Brooke's room.

When we get there, Randi and Jolene are sitting on the bed playing catch with the potato. Brooke is melting an ice cube on her arm. Meeka is sitting just inside the pagoda, cleaning her needles with a wet wipe.

Brooke looks up. *"Finally,"* she says.

"Yeah, this is getting seriously boring," Randi says, tossing me the potato.

This time I catch it.

Randi rolls off Brooke's bed and crawls past Meeka to get inside the pagoda. Jolene follows along. Stacey reaches for the CD player and turns off the music. "Guys," she says. "There's something I need to tell you."

"*Now* what?" Brooke asks. She holds the ice cup to her forehead like she's getting a headache.

Stacey glances at me, then back at the girls. "Ida doesn't want to do this dare," she says.

"Of course she doesn't want to do it," Brooke says. "That's the point of a dare."

Stacey crosses her arms. "Then we should think of a *new* dare," she says. "Because this one is too mean."

Brooke's mouth drops open. "*Mean?*" She huffs. "We built her a *pagoda*. Meeka sterilized her needles. I'm donating a pair of my best earrings." Brooke takes one of her melting ice cubes out of the cup. "I don't call that mean." She pops the ice into her mouth and crunches.

I glance at the other girls, but they don't look back at me. It's like I've shrunk to the size of the potato in my hand. Maybe even smaller.

This is the size I'll always be to them, I think to myself, *if I don't do this dare.*

My eyes still sting, but I blink it away and take

a breath. The air tastes like lip gloss and gummy bears and sweet pea body spritz. It tastes like fourth grade.

"Um . . ." I say quietly. "I think I panicked a little. I'm okay now. Let's do it."

Stacey lifts her eyebrows and looks at me. "Are you sure?"

I nod.

Brooke swallows her ice and smiles.

Meeka picks up her pincushion.

I squeeze my potato.

"Last one in is a rotten egg!" Randi hollers from inside the pagoda. Jolene scrambles past Meeka. Brooke and Stacey dive for the pagoda, giggling.

I get in line behind them.

"Wait!" someone suddenly shouts from the hallway. "*Waaaait!*"

Meeka looks up from her needles. Brooke and Stacey peek back out. I stop and turn.

Jenna rushes into the room. I didn't even know she was gone.

Brooke crawls back out of the pagoda. "Jenna Drews," she snaps. "You can't make us wait. *I'm* in charge, not you."

"Not hardly," Jenna says. She glances over her shoulder.

Jade steps into the room.

She studies the pagoda.

The cup of ice in Brooke's hand.

The pincushion in Meeka's.

The potato in mine.

Then she narrows her eyes. "What are you nut bars doing?"

"Uh-oh," I hear from deep inside the pagoda. "Not good."

Brooke steps past me. "We're piercing Ida's ears," she says to her sister. "Not that it's any of your business."

Jade zeroes in on Brooke. "You're *what*?"

Brooke huffs impatiently. "We're piercing Id—"

"I heard you," Jade cuts in. She studies all of us again. Then she shakes her head and groans. She snatches up Meeka's pincushion and holds it in front of Brooke's face. "These are *sewing* needles, pea brain."

Brooke does a small snort. *"Du-uh,"* she says.

Jade moves in even closer and locks eyes with her sister. "They're for fixing holes," she says. *"Not* piercing ears."

Brooke shrinks back a step. "But I heard Meghan tell you about her cousin. How she pierced her ears for her and—"

"If you're going to dip into other people's conversations," Jade interrupts, "then you better keep your pretty little ears tuned in for the whole thing."

Brooke twitches and her ice cubes clink. "W-what do you mean?"

"You missed the part about Meghan's cousin getting a major infection. They had to take her to the emergency room so the doctors could drain the *pus*."

"Eew!" we all say.

"Cool," slips from the pagoda.

"She had to have her head wrapped like a mummy for a *week,*" Jade continues.

Brooke shifts a little. "I must have missed that part."

Jade grabs the cup of ice out of Brooke's hand and plunks the pincushion into it. *"No* ear piercing," Jade says. "Not on my watch."

Jade sweeps past Jenna and down the hall. A moment later we hear her bedroom door slam.

Brooke just blinks for a minute. Then her

eyes slowly shift to Jenna. "*You* spilled the beans," she says. Her voice sounds as sharp as Meeka's needles.

Jenna doesn't flinch. She just lifts her chin. "*Someone* had to."

Brooke doesn't reply.

No one does.

No one even moves. It's like our feet have frozen to the floor.

Then I hear a rustling sound.

A shaggy head pokes out of the pagoda.

"I'm starved," Randi says. "When do we eat?"

We don't dare leave Brooke's room, so we huddle in the pagoda, eating the grapes Jolene brought, and waiting for Jade to cool down.

"What about Ida's dare?" Randi asks, popping a grape into her mouth. "Do we do it or not?"

"I vote not," I say.

"But we have to do something," Brooke says.

"Jade took my needles," Meeka says. "So it will have to be a substitute dare."

"Maybe something that gets back at Jade," Randi says. "For spoiling our daremony."

"*Jenna* is the one who spoiled it," Brooke says.

Randi shrugs. "Then Jenna can do the dare too. Two birds, one stone. Easy cheesy."

"Fine," Jenna says.

"Okay," I say. "But afterward, everything goes back to normal and nobody gets left out of the group. Deal?"

"Deal," everyone says together.

"Ooo . . . I've got an idea for their dare," Stacey says. She picks up Randi's potato and looks at me and Jenna. "You guys have to hide this in Jade's room!"

"But Jade's *in* her room," Jolene says. "They would have to be invisible."

"Plus, they would get seriously murdered," Meeka adds. "That's so not healthy."

"Okay, not in her room," Stacey says. "Just in her shoe or her coat or something."

Everyone agrees. Not because it's the best triple-dog dare ever, but because sometimes you just have to take what you get and move on before you get bored to death.

A few minutes later, we all listen at the door while Brooke asks Jade if we can please play ghosts in the graveyard. She uses her sweetest voice. The one Jade taught her for getting her way.

Brooke flies back to us. "It's a go," she says. "But if we break anything Jade will make us sleep in a snowbank. I'll be the ghost first so I can turn off the lights downstairs. You guys do the chant and then come looking for me. Ida and Jenna, you hide the potato in Jade's coat pocket while everyone is running around. It's in the closet by the front door."

"How will we know which coat?" Jenna asks.

"Don't worry," I say. "I've seen it before."

Brooke takes off and we start chanting slowly, to give her enough time to hide. "One o'clock . . . two o'clock . . . three o'clock . . . four o'clock . . ." When we get to "Midnight!" we all shout, "We hope we see a ghost tonight!"

Everyone scatters down the hallway, looking for Brooke. Jenna picks up the potato. "Follow me," she says.

"Wait," I say, grabbing her arm. "There's something I want to do first."

I take the potato from Jenna and walk over to Brooke's desk. I find a marker and write *Thanks a lot* on the potato. Only I don't write it in a mean way.

Jenna reads the potato and smirks. "Very thoughtful," she says.

"Yep," I say back. "Plus, I wanted to thank you too, for spilling the beans to Jade. That was really nice of you."

Jenna twitches. "I wasn't doing it to be nice," she says. "I just wanted to get back at Brooke for taking over my truth or dare game in the first place."

"Still," I say. "You were being a good friend when you did it."

Jenna huffs and looks away. "I'm not anybody's friend. *Frenemy* maybe, but not friend."

I do the huff too. "Then you were being a good *frenemy*. My *best* frenemy."

Jenna glances at me. And smiles.

We hear a fake scream and then the sound of feet pounding up the stairs. "C'mon," I say. "Let's get this dare over with so we can play too."

Jenna nods.

I lead the way.

Dear Stella,

I just got home from Brooke's sleep-over. I was supposed to get my ears pierced there, but things didn't go as planned. Jenna told Jade what we were up to and Jade made us stop. She was pretty mad, but she didn't tell on us.

She didn't finish doing our makeup either. I guess that was fair.

Stacey thought up a substitute dare for me and Jenna to do. It was the only one we did all night. I think we're done playing that game for a while.

There's a knock on my door. Mom looks in. "I forgot to tell you that Mrs. Drews called for you earlier."

"For me?"

Mom nods and walks over to me. She picks up George and sits down on my bed. "She needs a favor."

I blink and wait for more information.

"She has a doctor's appointment next Thursday when Jenna is at dance and she needs someone to watch Rachel. She wondered if you would babysit for her."

"Babysit? Why didn't she just ask you? I mean, you'll be home anyway, right?"

"Yes, I'll be here," Mom says. "But Rachel wanted *you*."

"Me?"

Mom nods. "Mrs. Drews said she'll pay you. Five dollars an hour."

I do a gasp. "She'll *pay* me? Just for watching Rachel? What did you tell her?"

Mom sets George on my lap. "I told her you might be busy because you always meet Stacey after dance on Thursdays."

I think about how much I like meeting Stacey and sharing a cookie and talking about best friend stuff. But sometimes plans change. Sometimes friendships do too. Even mine and Stacey's has been changing lately. Not in a bad way, like Brooke and Jenna's. Just in a different way. Maybe even a good way. Because even though I still like Stacey, I know I'm not exactly like her. And that's okay.

"I'll do it," I say. "Stacey owes me a skip anyway."

"Better call Mrs. Drews then," Mom says, standing up. "Her number's by the kitchen phone."

I set George by my journal and head downstairs.

"Everything good?" Mom asks when I hang up the phone. She looks up from the lettuce leaves she's rinsing in the sink.

I lean against the counter. "Everything's great," I reply. "Mrs. Drews said she might need me to babysit next weekend too, when Jenna's at Girl Scouts."

"Wow," Mom says, turning off the water and shaking the leaves. "You'll be rich."

"I know."

Mom sets the lettuce in a salad bowl and starts tearing it into pieces. I pick up a leaf and start tearing too. The whole time my brain is churning up an idea.

A great big idea.

"Mom?" I finally say. "Do I have to save my babysitting money, or can I spend it on whatever I want?"

Mom narrows her eyes. "That depends on what the *whatever* is."

I pause, daring myself to tell her.

"I want to get my ears pierced," I say. "As soon as possible."

"Ida," Mom says, "we've already talked about this."

"I know," I say. "You want me to wait until I'm ten. But I'm nine and a half now. And Mr. Crow says you always round half numbers *up*. So, if you do the math right, I'm already ten."

Mom does a little snort.

"I'll do all my chores," I continue. "With no reminders. And I'll take good care of Rachel. And after I get my ears pierced I'll clean them ten times a day so you won't have to take me to the emergency room."

Mom snorts again. Then she's quiet for a minute.

"Well . . ." she finally says. "I'll talk it over with Dad. And . . . if it sounds good to him—"

I don't wait to hear the end of this conversation.

I dive in, hugging her.

Mom rests her chin on top of my head and hugs me back.

☙

Jenna walks with me and Rachel to my house on Tuesday afternoon.

"This makes two weeks in a row," I say to Jenna as we head up my porch steps. "It's getting to be like a pattern with you."

Jenna gives me a squint.

"Yeah," Rachel says, taking my hand. "A big fat pattern."

"I'm just doing it to be fair," Jenna says. "Since you have to babysit Rachel while I'm at dance."

"I don't mind," I say.

"Yeah, Ida doesn't mind," Rachel adds. "She would babysit me every day if she could." Rachel looks up at me. "Right?"

"Right," I say back. "But what I meant was, I don't mind if Jenna comes to my house."

"You don't?" Jenna says.

"You don't?" Rachel chimes in.

"Nope," I say, opening the front door. "We can work on our snowflakes."

Mr. Crow showed us how to make paper snowflakes in school today. We get extra credit if we make more at home to hang in our classroom.

"Of course," Jenna says, following us inside. "I'm excellent at making them."

I find paper and scissors for both of us after Rachel starts her lesson. We sit on my bedroom floor and fold and cut the paper like Mr. Crow taught us, so that our snowflakes will be perfect hexagons when we unfold them again.

"We should cut the holes in geometric shapes," Jenna says. "Triangles. Circles. Squares."

I nod. "Maybe even stars."

"Maybe even *hearts*," Jenna adds. "Then you could give a snowflake to your *crush*."

"Ha, ha," I say. "I barely even like any boys."

Jenna snips at her snowflake for a minute. "I like Tom," she says.

My mouth drops. "Tom Sanders? But you made him drink his science experiment!"

Jenna rolls her eyes. "That was in first grade, Ida. I'm way more mature now." Jenna unfolds her snowflake. Little squares are scattered over its six points. "What about you?" she asks. "Who do *you* like?"

I think about what I wrote in my journal way back when I started it. About liking Quinn. And how I haven't told anyone that secret. Not even Stacey.

"I told you who I like, so you have to tell me who you like," Jenna says, folding a new sheet of paper. "It's only fair."

I cut heart shapes along the edge of my snowflake. "Maybe I like Quinn," I mumble. "A little."

Jenna snorts. "I knew it."

"How did you know?"

"Duh, Ida," she says, glancing up at me. "Remember when we built our snow fort and you hit Quinn with a snowball and he smiled at you?"

"You saw that?"

"Yup," Jenna says. "You turned ten shades of red."

I do a huff. "I did not turn colors!"

Jenna snorts again. "Like a box of crayons."

"If my cheeks were red, it was only because it was cold out," I say.

"Uh-huh," Jenna says back, cutting a circle in the center of her snowflake. "Don't worry. Your secrets are safe with me."

I unfold my snowflake and I give her half a smile. "Yours too."

Epilogue

Dear Stella,

We finished our math unit in school yesterday, so everyone helped Mr. Crow put away the little table of cardboard shapes and roll up the rug and hand back our concrete poems. He also let us take down our paper snowflakes if we wanted to keep them.

I took down the one I made with heart shapes and Jenna dared me to give it to Quinn. She's still the only one who knows that I like him. So I gave it to him even though we're not supposed to do dares in school.

Quinn grunted and stuck it in his desk.

Boys.

I glance up from my journal and see my reflection in the mirror that hangs behind my bedroom door. It's the million and oneth time I've looked at myself today.

Mostly just my ears.

Mostly just my earlobes.

That's because I counted all my babysitting money this morning and there was enough to get them pierced.

The more I tilt my head, the more my earrings sparkle. "They're my birthstone," I say to George. He's watching me from my dresser. "*Peridot*," I add, sliding off my bed and walking over to him. "Which I think is the artistic name for *green*."

George glances from my ears to my fish tank and I tap on the glass. "I'll clean your filter in a minute, Pic," I say to my fish. "Right after I clean my ears."

Pic must be happy to hear this, because he takes a couple of laps around the pirate.

I set George on my bed and glance at the picture of me and Stacey that's sitting on my nightstand. I called her this morning to see if she could go to the mall with me to get my ears pierced.

But she was on her way to Brooke's house to practice their dance for the spring recital.

So I called Jenna and asked her if she could go with me instead.

She said yes.

After the piercing lady cleaned my earlobes and marked them with two tiny dots, and held an earring shooter up to my ear, and said, "Ready?" I looked at Jenna and asked her if I could squeeze her hand.

She said, "Squeeze the blood out of it. I don't care."

So I did.

Which was a good thing because guess what? It hurts to get your ears pierced.

I pick up my journal again.

> I got my ears pierced today. Afterward we walked around the mall until I could breathe normally again. Then my mom got a coffee while me and Jenna looked around the Mish Mosh. Mom had given me some extra money so I could buy something for Jenna, to thank her for coming along.

We dug through the jewelry bin together
for a long time until she found exactly what she
wanted.

Ladybug barrettes.

Bye,
Ida